Saving Becky
Safe and Secure Book 6
Alyssa Bailey

Description

He was a deadly operative, but she called him Daddy.
As a former military pilot turned security operative, Carter has always been in control. But when he falls in love with the enchanting and efficient Becky, his boss's assistant, everything changes. His Daddy Dom comes out in force, but holding the reins steady is challenging some days when Becky smiles so sweetly. Suddenly, he's protecting more than just his clients - he's protecting his heart.

Just as their relationship begins to deepen, it is first stalled by Carter's secret, then Carter's plane is sabotaged, quickly followed by attempts on Becky's life. With danger lurking around every corner and Becky trying her best to solve the mystery on her own, Carter must rely on his skills and his team to ensure Becky's safety because the danger may be closer than they think.

Love the inside scoop? Sign up for my Newsletter with special offers and bonus content.
https://www.alyssabaileyromance.com

Alyssa Bailey
Saving Becky

Print ISBN: 979-8-9871524-3-0

Cover Design by Joe Dugdale
Edited by Marybeth Renn

Chapter 1

Becky stared at the aesthetically bland building she worked in. The interior gave you the impression of efficiency in the lap of luxury, but the outside was as plain as they came. Nice building, but you'd never know that an entire network of highly trained badasses worked and played within those dark brown brick walls. And she organized them all as Jacquard's personal assistant.

Jacquard and Associates seemed to have no problem getting into each other's business, which was odd for a predominantly male-dominated workplace, but Becky noticed they were cautious regarding each other's private lives. Recently, it seemed everyone was especially careful with her and Carter's saga. Relationships were delicate, and no one wanted to make a mistake by sticking their nose in too far. Becky knew she didn't want to make a mistake either, but here they were, and it felt like mistakes were everywhere.

"What are you doing for lunch, baby?"

Startled, Becky sighed deeply and looked up into her beloved's large blue eyes. Carolina blue, if she wasn't mistaken. Not as gray as her father's West Point uniform, but close. He was a big man, both in size and in spirit, a quality she had always admired about him.

Carter Brackovich was strong, confident, and a true alpha male that never seemed to back down from a challenge. Yet, here he was now, avoiding her gaze and looking away into the distance, a distance that seemed to grow increasingly with each passing day they didn't deal with their issues.

She gave Carter a half-shrug. "I don't know. Do you have any ideas? Someplace we can talk, maybe?"

It was not a demand, but a sincere request from her heart. Carter had shut her out recently in that department and Becky felt sure he was avoiding their elephant in the room... it was destroying all the things that made them what they were. Becky wanted to spend the rest of her life with Carter and eventually have his children. But he had refused to do more than give her a *maybe*.

Well, he had actually said not now, and that had hurt. She didn't want to marry Carter and later found out that *not now* meant *not ever*. She wasn't going to jump his bones until he got her pregnant, but she didn't want to wait much longer, so every day, she took her birth control.

She hated she couldn't just trust him because she trusted him in everything else, but in this, she was demanding proof, assurances, and for what? If she couldn't believe him in this, then why were they thinking of marriage?

Becky had asked *him* to marry *her* the last time they had this discussion. He had already asked her a few times over the last couple of years, but she had hesitated because she wanted children, and she was feeling the ticking of her biological clock louder every month that went by that ended with her menses.

"Why won't you agree to marriage?" he had asked. "We can get married and work out the rest later."

Her voice, barely above a whisper, responded. "Because I need to know we will have children. If you don't know, then how can I know that it will happen? I don't know why that is so important to me, but it is. Why can't you commit to even one baby?"

He didn't answer immediately, and when he finally spoke, his words came out slowly and deliberately.

"I'm just not ready yet," he said. "I want to be sure before I make any commitments, especially with children. Our children need to trust that I'm all in. You don't know what it's like..." He shook his head in what? Despair? Uncertainty? *Join the club.*

Becky's soulful sigh of disappointment spoke of her aching heart. She knew there was something more to his hesitation, something he wasn't telling her. She wanted to press him like he would press her if there were something she was holding back, but she knew it wouldn't do any good. He was holding this fear, this pain, close to his chest. Her thoughts went rampant, trying to fill in the blank for the source of his hesitation, but none of it made enough sense to be the whole reason.

She reached out and touched his arm gently. "Will you ever be ready?" she asked, her voice filled with quiet desperation.

He looked away, and she knew the answer before he even spoke.

"I don't know," he whispered, his voice tortured. "I want to say yes, but we have honesty between us, and I can't do that right now."

Becky had asked Carter many times before about why, when he was so good with kids, and he obviously loved them that he would be so hesitant about having one of his own. He had never opened up to her about the real reason for his fear.

Until he felt safe enough to tell her the real problem, then there wasn't anything she could do.

She now grasped the frustration Carter had when Becky held back the information he needed to make life better. How many times had she done that with Carter, even when he had said how much it hurt things when she didn't trust him enough to share? Nonetheless, after showing her the error of her ways, Carter loved her even more. That was what she was determined to do.

Becky wished Carter could, but something was stopping him. At least he hadn't shut her down completely this time. She drew hope from that change. As Carter reached to open the door of his Escalade for her, Becky heard his phone go off. The face he made as he pulled the device from his pocket made Becky smile as she shook her head. They weren't getting their lunch together. He barely held his irritated response inside as he spoke in deep hushed tones, walking as he talked. He was a quick processor, unlike herself, that liked to review all systems before making her response.

Becky knew this Carter, he was the most patient man of any of the team, but he had his limits of what he could tolerate, and he'd sought her out for lunch. He didn't like his plans interrupted even though thinking on his feet was another well-known strength of his. He was usually very accurate. That was why Monroe, who was a brilliant strategist, worked well with Carter, who loved boots and, when necessary, decisions on the ground.

"Sorry, baby. I'm being called into service to fly Levi and Kaden to meet up with their next assignment. Seems they are paying extra to get security up to them quickly."

"It's okay. Will you be back tonight?"

"Yeah. Shouldn't be more than a few hours in the air both ways and a couple on the ground. I'll miss dinner, though."

Becky opened her mouth to reply, and Carter swooped down to kiss her deeply, the strength of which took her breath away. Carter was breathing hard as well when he lifted his head and grinned. "Think that will hold my place until I get back and finish the job?"

"I think it might, but no overnights because then you will owe me." Her giggle had him rearranging his cock with a grimace and she wiggled in arousal. "I'll just go get my car and grab some lunch. Don't forget to get yourself something. You know how you are when you haven't eaten enough."

"Don't worry about me. I'm a big boy but I don't want my girl out alone. I have a feeling that is making my gut rumble. And no," he lifted his brow giving her the *don't be naughty* look, "it isn't because I'm hungry. How about ordering in today?"

"You never like me ordering takeout."

He nodded and sighed. "I know, but I have this odd feeling in my gut about leaving you alone today."

Becky knew Carter's gut was a real thing, and she had learned to listen as much as he did to it. She nodded. "Okay."

"Daddy. Okay, Daddy."

"You're kind of needy today, my Teddy Bear. And bossy." Carter raised his eyebrow again. "Fine. Just for you, Daddy. Ow! Not at work, Carter," she hissed as she resisted rubbing the sting off her butt.

"At work, in the grocery store, at the house. You cop an attitude with me, and I'll pop that little butt."

Becky shifted in place. Her arousal was making her slick and her core heat up. She murmured as she walked away about her not-so-little butt.

"That's ten. There is nothing bad to be said about my Baby Bear."

She loved it when he used endearments with her as he often did. Baby Bear was his most loved name for her, and since she assured others that he was a teddy bear when they commented on his size, she naturally became Baby Bear.

"I have to pick up Levi and head out. I can't assume how long I'll be, but of course, I can't be positive that I'll be home tonight. I'll make sure to let you know when I know." He reached his hand out to caress her face. "I love you with all that I am."

She gave him a half smile. "I know."

Carter leaned down and cuddled her before kissing long enough to make her feel the slightest bit dizzy. He was the best kisser. It was foreplay and aftercare in one. Every. Damn. Time. Becky watched as he grabbed his kit from the back seat, opening it, and doing a quick mental inventory before he kissed her quickly and nudged her toward the office entrance.

Carter went on overnight jobs with some regularity. Becky sometimes liked solitude and tried to imagine life alone, without Carter, without her Daddy. She couldn't. She didn't want to live without him. Maybe he had a genetic or hereditary thing that made him afraid to have children. They could adopt. She shook her head as she watched from inside the building's front doors as Carter left the parking lot. She was grasping at straws and that wasn't a good idea. Too many wrong conclusions happened when one did that.

This issue was something to ponder another day because it was time to grab a quick lunch before going back to work. Carter was going to be gone for hours and she would likely have to have not only lunch but dinner and maybe even breakfast alone. Her bottom cheeks clenched as she walked over to her car and climbed in. She had just enough time to grab enough lunch to have it for dinner too.

If she hurried, and settled for curry, she could get there and back before it was time to work, and if there was one thing Rebecca Shea Carrington always did, it was to show up on time. She might not see her boss Jac for most of the day, or sometimes not at all, but she was where he needed her to be, and that was often in the office.

While she waited for her double order, she got a text from Carter.

Carter: "What are you having for lunch?"

Becky: "Curry. Should I order enough for dinner?"

Carter: "For one. I'll grab something on my way home. Sorry, Baby Bear."

Becky: "Okay. Hey, my order is here."

Carter: "Well, you better go and get it then. And enjoy it because it cost you ten swats."

Becky: "What?"

Carter: "Look at the drive-thru."

She leaned over to look out of the window. Busted. What could she say? Nothing.

Becky: "Sorry, Daddy."

Carter: "Too late for that. I've caught you. Hope it's great curry. Now get your lunch and get right back to work. Don't stay late and have the front desk security walk you to your car tonight. And before you say anything," Becky imagined his voice growing deeper, "Don't forget you have twenty on the books already."

Shoot.

Becky: "Yes, Daddy. Stay safe."

Carter: "I will baby, see you at least for breakfast." Her belly flipped and she needed fresh panties. Maybe she should do what Sharlee did and keep a few pairs at the office.

When Becky drove into the underground parking garage, Jac was leaning against the elevator wall, arms crossed over his chest. He was a nice-looking man, but Becky only had eyes for one man, and it looked like that man had called her boss to meet her. Jac smiled when she pulled in.

Walking to the driver's side of the car, he opened the door for her when she turned off the vehicle.

"Don't tell me."

"Been a bit naughty I hear. Not typical for my assistant so I'm surprised but expect, when Carter comes home, he'll take care of that issue. Come and eat your lunch. You have just enough time to do that and get ready for our next meeting with your favorite people."

Becky groaned as they entered the elevator. "Can't I sit this one out?"

"Nope, I need you there, and that FBI agent enjoys it better when you are there. I get him so confused that I get my way before he figures out that he has been bested."

"Jac, I'm not sure that's very ethical." Becky laughed.

"Maybe not, but hey, those alphabet agencies are underhanded, too."

"True," said Becky as she sat the curry on the desk.

JUST AS THE MEETING was ending, Jac's phone rang.

"Reynaud." Jac stiffened. "Where are you?" He placed his hand over the receiver. "Get Garrett and Monroe here and call Sharlee. I want them ready to receive a call from me."

Sharlee was calling before Becky got to the phone while Jac was still talking into his cell. Becky ended the video meeting in Jac's office and answered his desk phone.

"Sharlee?"

"Becky, I'm triangulating on the plane, and I'll watch so if they go down, we will know exactly where to grab them from."

"When who goes down? Oh, God, is Carter's flight in trouble?"

Everyone in Jacquard and Associates was hard working, hard playing, and super intense when a situation was going FUBAR. Those times didn't happen often because they were well-trained men in well-rehearsed situations. When things did seem to fall apart, even when he sent others home to rest, Jac didn't go home.

Over the years, she'd found him bent over his desk the next morning, still worrying about a problem, or watching his team in a tricky situation. Since he had married Sharlee, he did that mother-hen behavior from home more than in the office. But he still did it. Tonight was one of those times.

Before too long, everyone who wasn't already committed or out on a job had assembled in Jac and Becky's offices and the adjoining conference room. It was early yet, but Jac had canceled his staff meeting and the support staff continued to work not knowing that three of the company's agents were in a situation. The women all showed up for support. Finley, Storm's nanny, stayed home with Storm and Sharlee, who didn't dare leave her computer.

Ivy sat close to Becky. Mallory, who seemed to be the most maternal of them all, fussed over the women and kept them occupied. Callie was more in the role of operative than one of the girls right now which left Mallory to do what needed doing. The guys and Callie were in a huddle working on possible exfil solutions if needed.

When Garrett came over to check on the women, Becky asked, "Why don't we know anything?"

Garrett, like the others, was incredibly protective of Becky because she was the first female employee in the company. She was special but so were all the women. He grabbed her hand. "Because your man is an excellent pilot. He is doing what he has to do to get the plane down safely. The closer to his destination he can get, the better."

"But what happened?" she asked for the tenth time in the last hour.

Monroe walked up and sat on the other side of Ivy and took hold of her hands in his and massaged them absently. Ivy had gone silent, and Becky was worried about her.

Monroe spoke. "We don't actually know. Carter will tell us more when this is over. The one thing we do know is Carter, Levi, and Kaden have been through things like this before. They are well versed in how to handle emergencies and if they know you girls are okay, then they will be able to concentrate on dealing with the problem at hand."

"I know," said Ivy in a low voice. "Kaden says he'll do fine if he knows I'm safe. He knows I'm safe, right?"

"He does, honey. Just as he trusts us to take care of you girls, trust them to take care of business and get back home safe and sound." Ivy nodded and went back to being quiet.

Becky, however, looked at Garrett who stood back a little now, and said, "So, how long before we know?"

Jac walked up to the small group, and Mark, Callie, and a couple of Levi's old team joined them. "They've landed safely." Jac looked at Becky and Ivy.

"How did he do it? Where are they?" asked Becky.

"Carter made it happen somehow. He found an area that might have been used for a landing strip some years ago and he touched down there. Thing is, they're about forty klicks or twenty-five miles from where they were going."

"And it'll be dark in a few hours," added Becky, understanding the decision they needed to make.

"So, what's going to happen?" asked Ivy.

Jac went down on his haunches, like Garrett had with Becky and she marveled at the family they had built with this group of men and women. She was proud of who they were and what they represented. The best of the best. Jac looked into Ivy's frightened eyes. "We are going to keep them there and go pick them up bright and early tomorrow morning."

"Carter won't leave his plane," said Becky with absolute assurance.

Garrett grunted. "No, he won't. Since we don't have much time before dark, we are going to leave them there overnight, on the plane, and give him a chance to work on the problem. Kaden will continue to be our eyes and ears as to how they are doing, and Levi will make it comfy for the night."

"But it's cold up there," said Ivy.

"Ivy," said Monroe, "they have enough supplies to last a few weeks, so a few hours will be easy."

Suddenly, on the wall, Kaden appeared. "Hey guys, this is the best I can do to communicate directly with everyone. Ivy, honey, don't worry about this little overnight stop. We are cozy and have plenty of what we need. I'll see you tomorrow and I love you." His voice got firm. "Stay with someone tonight. I don't want you to worry when you are by yourself."

"Okay. I love you too." Ivy seemed to relax once she heard Kaden's voice.

Carter's head appeared in the frame. "Hey, Baby Bear. I'm going to work on the plane and see if I can figure out what went wrong. Be good and Kaden is right, you shouldn't stay alone so buddy up with someone. I love you."

"I will and I love you too, so much. See you tomorrow."

Levi came on briefly, gave some updates on things Becky didn't even have a clue about and was gone. The screen disappeared.

"Okay, who's going home with me?" asked Mallory.

"You know, if Ivy doesn't mind, I think we'll just spend the night together. We live very close, and it's just another overnight with the guys in less-than-optimal accommodations," stated Becky.

Ivy nodded.

Mark laughed. "Are you kidding? They are not in enemy territory, not on a hush hush mission, and they are inside an airtight, watertight plane. I'd say they are only missing their girls tonight. I know that's a big deal but under the circumstances, they are going to kick back and enjoy the evening pretty well."

"You're right. I think we'll head out and settle in for the night. Maybe a hot tub night is in order, eh Ivy?"

Mark started gathering his gear. "No hot tub if you two are alone. You'll crank it up, drink wine, and then be too tipsy to know what you're doing and could drown. No hot tub."

The women stared at Mark and the room went silent. Then they burst out laughing.

"Man, Jessie better hurry and have this kid. You are losing it," said Garrett, shaking his head.

Mark smiled sheepishly. "Don't I know it."

Monroe and Mallory talked for a few minutes and then Mallory spoke. "I'll stay with you two if you think it would help."

"Thanks, Mal, but I just don't think it is a big deal now we know they are safe on the ground. Go home. We'll be fine."

Grabbing her gear and the extra curry from the fridge, Becky and Ivy went to Becky's house. As the evening wore on, Ivy relaxed. Likely the too much Pinot Noir wine and the one glass of Carter's whiskey she'd consumed contributed to the lighter mood, but she'd eaten, so Becky let her go. She didn't offer to open another bottle of wine. Ivy was fun and smart, with a glow about her when nothing was stressing her out. She was the youngest of the women, but she was finding her way.

Becky made Ivy take some pain reliever and drink water before leaving a few crackers and another bottle of water and more medicine on the side table in the guest room. Becky couldn't get to sleep. No surprise really, Carter wasn't home because he was in the woods in a situation not of his choosing, so she lay there and thought about things. When she was in college, she'd never thought she'd know people like these she worked and played with now. Danger wasn't in her vocabulary before signing on with Jac. Now, she slid past the word danger and assessed the level of risk.

As far as being a savvy businessman on the practical side of things, Jac wasn't any better than any other. He was good at hiring the best to take care of the paperwork side. He had hired Becky, who took care of the front end. Later, Jac hired Sharlee, who was a computer wizard and after what seemed like forever, the two powerhouses were an unstoppable force as a couple. Now they had added little Storm. Jac and Sharlee aptly named their son.

Becky remembered when Jac hired Jessie, the forensic accountant, to handle the backroom finances and protect the business' bottom line. Soon Mark was protecting Jessie in his home, and they were now waiting for their first miracle. Next came Ivy whom Kaden had met during a job that led them to Montana and later to deal with the mafia.

Then there was Mallory for Monroe, who met at a lifestyle gathering and things went from there. Monroe was a Daddy to Mallory who, like Becky, enjoyed being lovingly dominated by their mate. Finally, Callie, who had been with Garrett after Sharlee arrived but before Jessie, had disappeared and then reappeared in Garrett's life. It had been rough going, and Becky had learned a lot about the dangers in government agencies, but things were fine now.

Now, she and Carter were better but had plenty of ups and downs. Becky was sure they would figure things out, but it wasn't easy going right now. The girls all said it was part of the forever process, but she hated it. It would be awkward if they were to end their relationship. Becky couldn't imagine working anywhere but in the same place with the man she loved. That's why she was determined that they would figure things out.

Still, if it came to doing this job and taking care of his people, and his family, you could never ask for someone better to have your back than this team. You had to be careful that, if you were a woman, it was only your protection on the line, not your backside for chastisement. However, since Sharlee, Jac had turned his close female employees over to their men for discipline. The rest got his particular brand of "look."

Jac was a demanding boss to work for sometimes, but he was always fair. She didn't always agree with him, because he was over-protective of the people he considered his family, but he had an uncanny insight into the needs of his people. Like Carter and the others on the original team, Jac read his gut like other people read the newspaper. Maybe Carter's gut was about him today and not her.

Like many men who worked with him, Carter believed in keeping his girl in line with a murmured reminder, a hand along the small of her back, the camber of her butt, or, when all else failed, a swat to the ass. Becky rarely felt Carter's hand anymore, for fun or discipline. She had to wonder if that was because it wasn't who he was now or maybe he was afraid to touch her. Or he didn't want that with her anymore. Didn't want to be her Daddy. But no, he had just made her call him Daddy. Somehow, she didn't think she had suddenly become the perfectly safe, careful woman Carter talked about but didn't actually want. He didn't like perfection and that was a good thing because she wasn't even close. Where was the fun in that, anyway?

When it came to Becky, Carter seemed hesitant in many ways. Punishments of the hands-off variety were never his style before. He was eager to swat her butt or twist a nipple. Now, he simply lifted his brow, patted her bottom, and murmured "Watch it" when she stepped out of line. There were no further repercussions. And she did it more often now to get his attention. Kaden said it was likely because Carter wanted to ensure he didn't step over Becky's boundaries too dramatically, but Becky wondered if that was true. Why now?

Carter never seemed to worry about boundaries when he had a mission or when there was something he wanted to get done. He would move the barrier to allow him to finish the job, whether it was barbecuing steaks, supporting his friends, or getting the job done. And she had no doubt he loved her. After today, the fear of losing him was bitter in her mouth. Fighting for them was the only way she knew.

If Carter would say... or do... *anything* as he used to when they had started their relationship, it would help. She sighed. It didn't help to dream about Carter being different because he didn't seem inclined to move the barrier this time. They had been together for almost two years now, and she knew he understood what she wanted, needed from him.

He was so romantic, loving, and kind, and he had taken control so she could let go sometimes, but right now, the occasional times he did, weren't enough. Carter had a Daddy persona, and you could see it a mile away, but only a couple of times had he used it with Becky as completely as she needed it these last months. It was as though he thought it would insult her or make her angry. Communication was the key here.

Mallory continued to encourage Becky to start a conversation. "Talk to him." So here she was, still holding onto this stupid contract, and she'd had it since the night Callie called into Jac and Sharlee's. When all that mess started with Garrett being a coldhearted wolverine, it ended with Callie staying. She and Garrett were happy again, more than before Callie left. Callie even talked about possibly looking for an older child to adopt. Pregnancy just wasn't for her, she said, nor babies.

But it was for Becky, and while adopting was fine, she was determined that if she didn't settle this with Carter once and for all soon, she'd have to end their relationship so she could find someone who wanted the same things she did, like children. It would break her heart, but better to break it now so she could rebuild it later with someone else, than break it forever with no children and no family.

Tonight, she had planned to negotiate as Mallory had suggested but here she was, alone in her bed, praying Carter and the guys would be home in the morning, no worse for the wear. Becky thought of Carter and the way he had brought her to a glorious climax this morning and then they had showered together. Grabbing her trusty vibrator from the side table drawer, she relived the morning and brought herself off in a modified glorious way. Before going to sleep hugging her teddy as a Daddy Bear substitute, she fell asleep determined to make what they had work. And hoping she would see Carter in the morning.

Chapter 2

I vy had classes to teach this morning, and after she had more water and tablets, she went home to have a long, hot shower, get dressed, and open up her studio. Jac called to inform the women that Carter had repaired the problem.

"Are you okay this morning?" asked Jac.

"I'm good. Ivy is not as good because she felt too good last night, but she'll be fine."

"Okay, Garrett sent in Levi and Kaden's replacements, and they are on their way back with a helicopter escort.

"Sounds good. Leave me their names so I can keep up. Did you go home last night?"

"I did. But I'm back early this morning to make sure everything was covered."

"You could have called me."

"I could have. If you are coming in, I'll fill you in on the rest later."

Because of the craziness of the afternoon before, Sharlee had come in to see if there was anything she could figure out by running an interfaced diagnostic on the plane once it was on the ground. She and Kaden would work on that while Levi caught a ride with the helicopter pilot back to the offices.

Becky's phone rang and she smiled as she read the caller ID. "Hey."

"Hey, Baby Bear. I'm back. Are you doing okay?" Carter's voice was calm and soothing, wrapping her like a warm fuzzy blanket, cuddling her in comfort.

Her voice trembled slightly from her need for him. *I'm not going to cry now.* "I'm good. I'm working right now but I missed you."

"I've still got some things to do here if you are able to hold out a few more hours. Then we'll go home and take a long shower and a nap."

"That sounds heavenly but... what if I need more?"

His deep, relaxed chuckle warmed her and made her tremble at the same time. "More, huh? Greedy today, baby? Me too. I think we should deal with that before the nap, yeah?"

"Yeah."

Another pair of panties for the laundry. She had to remember to carry extras.

Later, taking her morning break while waiting for Carter to finish and come find her, Becky walked down the hallway and checked on Sharlee, who had come in to work in the office. Sometimes Finley came with her and brought little Storm, who was walking now. Rounding the corner and entering the room, she felt her whole countenance brighten when she saw Storm and Jessie, who was big, round, and fussy pregnant.

"I can't believe I am still carrying this child in front of me instead of in my arms. Or better yet, in Mark's arms. I hope this isn't an indication that he or she isn't going to leave after they graduate high school and college."

Becky started to laugh but cut off fast when she saw the panicked look on Jessie's face. "I'm sure that won't be the case."

"It's not funny. This could be my forewarning. I will probably have a boy who never wants to leave home. It would be equally tragic if a girl didn't want to leave home, but I think Mark would have a hard time letting his daughter leave. And what does that make me? A terrible mother before he's even born?"

"Honestly," said Sharlee, "it doesn't mean anything. It means you have too many hormones to count, and everything seems like it could turn into a Greek tragedy. Have some chocolate. It helps."

"Are you kidding? If I show up with chocolate breath when Mark has been so careful that I eat only specific things these last couple of months, he will kill me. He's worried the baby won't gain the right weight, and if I eat junk, it will predispose him or her to battle fat cells. When I am healed from all of this, it will take a week before I can sit without a cushion, anyway."

Sharlee laughed. "Nothing you aren't used to."

"No, thank you. I'm waiting on unencumbered sex, and if I have to have a spanking before... oh... hand over the chocolate."

Becky wondered why Carter couldn't take charge of her more like his friends were with their spouses and girlfriends. Not that denying her chocolate would ever be okay, but still. She didn't need a bully because she would never stand for that, but sometimes...

But that wasn't Carter these days, and it seemed like it never would be again. She dreamed of the day that Carter would again take over for her. Not allow her to do for herself unless he agreed to it. She could give it all over to him and take a break. After a long day of dealing with work, sometimes she wanted that. Badly. She wondered if he'd ever be that person again and if she would be okay if he never was.

Carter's size, deep voice, and ability to practically snap people in half made him overly passive in social situations, and she knew it. But he seemed to have so much control, and every part of his life couldn't do this. It would fit so much into his caring mentality. She and the other ladies would have dinner at Ivy and Kaden's house. The guys were going to go over to Jac's. Maybe she would bring this up tonight with the ladies and see if they had any good ideas that wouldn't get them all sitting carefully.

She spent the rest of her break playing with the baby, discussing Jessie's new baby plans and Mallory's recently announced, who was still in the puking stage of pregnancy. Evidently, being a pharmacist didn't always help.

As Becky left to go back to the front desk, her cell was ringing, and her step got bouncier. That had to be Carter, and when she looked at her phone, she grinned. "Hey, where are you?"

"Looking for my wayward Baby Bear. She was supposed to be hard at work, but when I came to whisk her away, she was nowhere to be found."

"I took a break." She stepped into the room. "But I'm back. Jac is appointment free this afternoon so I can go when you're ready."

Carter opened his arms at the entrance to the office, and Becky walked into them. He was like a drug she never wanted to stop taking. His comforting hug absorbed the worry and fears of life without him. She released a sob that she tried to stifle, and she felt his hand slide behind her neck, under her shoulder-length hair.

"Hey, Baby Bear, it's okay. Daddy's here. No worries, I've got you. Daddy has to talk to Jac a little to bring him up to speed and then we'll go home and make this mess all feel better."

She nodded. "Uh-huh. I have to clear things up at my desk and set up for tomorrow, anyway." Carter waited until Becky began to pull away before releasing his hold on her. His kiss was gentle and claiming, just what she needed, causing her knees to grow weak with desire. He turned her in the direction of her desk with a playful swat while he headed in the direction of Jac's office beyond.

Carter rapped on the open doorframe and Jac immediately told him to come in. "Close the door."

Carter had a seat in front of Jac's desk. "Had a little adventure. If you wanted to go camping, we could have made a group trip of it."

Carter smiled. "Yeah, a spur-of-the-moment thing."

"Well, those aren't authorized, so cut it out," joked Jac. His face grew serious. "So, what happened up there?"

By the time they were wrapping the conversation up, the mechanic called. "Hey, Sam. What's the verdict?" Carter's expression hardened and he sat up. "Hold on. I'm putting you on speaker. I'm with Jac."

"Hey, Jac. Yeah, like I was saying, I suspect sabotage, but can I prove it? Probably not. See, the wiring to the internal GPS seems tampered with causing you to be off course a little when it vibrated loose, and that's what you found in the field. Luckily that was all that happened. The potential for greater damage was much worse because many of the wires and connectors were loose. I checked it myself after the last flight and I did an in-depth review of all systems. They weren't loose."

"Right, now what?" asked Jac.

"We fix it. It will take a while, so you aren't going to use your plane, Carter, until I'm done."

"Understood. Knowing what could have happened... well, you take your time," said Carter.

"Any way can we know if someone accessed the hangar?" asked Sam.

"We're a security company, we have eyes on everything except the bathrooms," said Jac. "The bigger problem now is whoever did it had a keycard, otherwise our sensors would have been going off. I think we upgrade security around there."

"Might be a good idea," said Sam. After a little more discussing and planning the call ended.

Carter said, "Grabbing Bec and going home."

Jac nodded. "See you two tomorrow."

Carter swooped Becky into his embrace, walking to the garage. "When we get home, drop your clothes and stand in the corner like the naughty girl you are."

"What?"

He dropped a kiss on her confused lips. "You owe me a curry run ten, ten for speaking badly about yourself and then hot sex."

"Mmm, yes, sir."

"I thought you'd agree."

IT HAD BEEN A LONG week. The break-in at the hangar got special attention. Carter had been working hard on a job and she was glad it was the end of the day on Friday. Becky looked at the clock as the call from the front desk came through. That didn't bode well because a five o'clock call to the office usually meant Jac had company. An unscheduled, late afternoon visitor, to be exact. She had spoken to the hunky guy on front desk duty today. If a woman was looking for distraction, this was the place to work. Becky smiled. It had worked out for her.

She frowned when she was informed that a Mr. Ramirez was at the front desk, insisting that he speak with Jac. Becky hadn't heard about him before, and security was keeping him at the entrance waiting to hear whether they would let him further into the building. There was yelling that someone couldn't do something she couldn't make out, and immediately following that, her office door opened to a dark-featured man of medium build, flanked by two men Jac would have liked to hire.

She put down the receiver and focused a stern, no-nonsense stare at the intruding, well-dressed man. "I'm sorry, but Mr. Reynaud is not seeing anyone else today. He has an opening Monday after lunch if you would like."

"That isn't going to work." He looked at her desk nameplate. "Ms. Carrington. Look at his schedule again. Maybe you didn't hear my name correctly. Martín Garcia Ramirez."

"Thank you, Mr. Ramirez, but it will not get you in to see Mr. Reynaud today. However, as I mentioned, he does have an... "

"No! I must see him today. It is a matter of," Mr. Ramirez lowered his voice, "life or death."

Becky knew this was very likely the truth. Jac rarely took unscheduled appointments from non-clients. There were a few federal agencies he hadn't blackballed. Very few. This man was not from a federal agency. He looked as though he was used to getting his way, and the two bodyguards with him were equally polished and demanding, but obviously the muscle.

"Let me check with Mr. Reynaud."

She buzzed Jac and explained the situation. At first, he told her they needed an appointment. Then a text flashed on her monitor screen. Jac was messaging her. "Does he have an accent?"

"A slight one."

"Two goons with him?"

"Yep."

"A scar on his right hand?"

Becky tried to lean just enough to see Mr. Ramirez's right hand. "Tell him yes, my dear." The gentleman held up his hand.

"Yes."

"Damn. Can't turn him away. Tell him to leave his guns with you and his goons in the outer waiting room. If he does, send him in. If he refuses... no, let me tell him."

Becky was relieved because she didn't have the chutzpah to stand up to this man who expected to be the dictator, not to be dictated to. The door opened behind her.

"Martín. You look well. Come in. Your friends must wait in the outer waiting room, and your guns can go in my safe. I'm surprised that my guy allowed you in with those."

"They are... different. Undetectable."

"I see. Becky, you may go for the evening. I imagine Mr. Ramirez won't mind."

"Not at all, my dear. I'm sure you have a husband to take care of."

"Her man is memorable. Go home, Becky." That shocked her. Becky? Twice? Jac had tried one day to call her Becky and that had been it. He was a full-name guy. So why? Something must be wrong.

"On my way, sir."

Something was going on. She needed to call Carter and Sharlee.

"Don't forget to tell Charlotte you're leaving."

Yep, that verified it. She never told Sharlee when she left work.

"Yes, sir. See you tomorrow." She turned to the demanding man who seemed to push Jac into a protective stance. "Nice to have met you, sir." As she prepared to walk out the door, she turned as if she had just remembered. "Mr. Reynaud, do you want me to tell Team One that you will be tied up and won't meet them at the gym today?"

"Looks like it, Becky. Thank you."

"I don't anticipate keeping you long," said Ramirez.

Jac nodded. "Tell them I'll be late."

"Right, sir." Becky left, went straight to the reception desk, and had them call the available Team One members while she called Carter. After a brief explanation, she headed to the tech room.

"Good call, baby. That Ramirez is a slimy dude," said Carter as he pulled her in for a quick kiss. "Now, let's get you on your way home and we'll stay to get some strategy going here."

"No way. I'm staying."

She crossed her arms over her chest and Carter worked hard to suppress his smile. He was almost successful. His girl was showing her naughty side and that was unusual and adorable.

Kaden pulled up Sharlee on the monitors. "Got your ears on?"

"Yep. I'll pipe it through."

Monroe said, "Carter, Garrett, and I will stroll down to Jac's office."

"I can go back and say I forgot something."

Carter turned into her and blocked her way to the exit. "No. You can stay, but you must stay here." He leaned down and spoke next to her ear. "Don't make me Daddy you in front of everyone."

The look she gave him was disbelief. Their dynamic was private. The lifted eyebrow and nod of his head said, *Believe it*. Unfortunately, her sassy self was having a hard time processing his message.

"I'm good, Carter. It's my job to back up Jac when he needs it. I have an excuse to knock on his door."

Carter's face grew hard as he leaned down, speaking low again so only she could hear. "If you want a hot ass for days, you will disobey me. I meant what I said. Do not leave this office unless it's with another member of our team or they will all know what it looks like when your Daddy shows up at work."

She looked up in the face of the man she hated to love sometimes and nodded.

"Let me hear it, Baby Bear."

She loved it when he called her that. Her knees always became weak, and he knew as well as she did that whatever he asked, she would do. "But Jac..."

"Is in good hands. You did your job. Now let us do ours. Say it."

Becky sighed. "Yes, sir."

Carter gave her a slight smile, nodded, and kissed her lips, which still showed her dissatisfaction with the situation. He whispered in her ear. "No pouting, baby. Daddy will be back to take you home." She nodded and watched the men leave.

Kaden and Becky watched on the monitors as Carter, Garrett, and Monroe entered Becky's office. Carter and Monroe sat in the outer waiting room with the two goons. Garrett, bold as only an original partner could be, knocked and then entered Jac's office, closing the door behind him.

The other monitor showed him being introduced to the man in Jac's office and Garrett sitting instead of leaving because Jac had a meeting in progress. Jac nodded at his visitor, but they didn't shake hands. The meeting ended quickly after that.

Jac opened his safe, pulled out the guns, and held them until he escorted the group out the door. Once Jac had accompanied the three men out of the building, careful not to acknowledge two of his men keeping company behind Ramirez's security, he handed over their weapons. Stepping back behind the bulletproof doors he watched them close before signaling to security who electronically locked them. Then more cameras inside and out came online, triggered by the locks. Then all four men walked to the tech room.

"I figured this is where you would all be. You there, Charlotte?"

"Yes, I'm here. I was able to record most of your meeting. Kaden monitored the outer office too."

Jac nodded. "Good."

Becky asked, "Who was that?"

Jac sighed. "That, my dear, is a long story I won't tell without whiskey."

"Come home, and I'll have the good stuff ready," said Sharlee.

"On my way." Jac looked tired but scrubbed his face with his hands and stood taller. "Let's get out of here. It looks like snow, and I want to get home. We'll deal with Ramirez later."

"Calling the girls. Levi and Mark are out of town right now on assignment," said Garrett. "I'll have Callie call them to see if they want to bunk up with someone."

"We wanted to have a girls' night out," complained Becky.

"Baby, you can do it tomorrow. Saturday is a better night anyway." Carter rubbed her back as she leaned into her sweet, bossy man.

"We were going to Ivy's place."

"And now you'll do it tomorrow." Carter's voice was taking on a decided edge.

Becky shook her head. "Can't. They are going somewhere this weekend."

Kaden spoke up from behind the group. "She's right. Maybe they can do it next week."

Becky pulled out of Carter's arms and walked off. Carter let her go, and for some reason, Becky wanted to cry because of it. She was a mess. Lately, she had difficulty spending time with Jessie and Mallory. They were pregnant, and Becky ached to have a baby so badly that it hurt her heart to be near them for too long. How could she be happy for them and resentful at the same time?

All of that emotional confusion, Carter working late all week, the incident last week, Ramirez tonight, and the recent discovery that her dad's inventory was incredibly off this close to tax time had been too much. She'd acted the petulant child and she'd known it, but she wanted Carter to take over and he hadn't done that in a real way for entirely too long. Stomping and crying was the only thing she knew to do.

Becky heard a text notification. She glanced at the message, but her tears blurred her vision too much. Wiping them away and trying to stem the flow, she could finally read the screen. It was from Ivy. Becky leaned against her car and read it.

"Hey, are you coming over tonight?"

Becky sighed and then replied. "The guys said we weren't having our get-together tonight."

"You leave that up to me. See you at seven."

Serves those guys right, but now she didn't know if she wanted to go. Carter didn't get to dictate to her if he wasn't willing to Daddy her, be her husband, or make babies with her. Except he was pretty heavy into the Daddy zone just a little bit ago. Could it be that he didn't want them with her? It sounded far-fetched, but who knew, anymore? And she hated that she was obsessed with this issue, but she was.

With renewed determination and eagerness to get home to change out of her work clothes, which were usually like the guys when they were on assignment, business grade attire but she had the addition of pumps, and her feet were killing her. She heard a man on the phone as she reached down to grab the handle of her car door.

It wasn't Carter because he hadn't followed her. She listened momentarily and heard something she knew she wasn't supposed to hear. Ramirez was talking to the men he'd brought with him and someone on the other end of the phone line while wisps of gray cigarette smoke curled from the partially open window. The phone was on speaker.

"Reynaud is playing hardball. If he doesn't want to help us, we will need to convince him he does."

"Why can't we just go to another security company? There are lots of bodyguard places that don't care about the reason behind the job."

"Because Reynaud is the best. His people aren't only vetted; they have experience and training that is second to none. The problem is they also come with ethics, and business is so good they will turn down even the generous offer I made him, if it's against his morality line."

One of the goons in the SUV said, "We could do the job. Want us to mess him up for you? It'd be child's play."

Ramirez laughed. "You would not come out of that well in either case. No, I have other ways to convince him that this job is one he wants to accept. I can't afford for him not to take this job." He took his phone off speaker. "Now let's go. I've got another meeting to attend."

The luxury SUV started to pull out. When Becky turned to verify who was talking, her eyes slammed into the steady gaze of Ramirez's black eyes. He stared for a second longer and then nodded before the car pulled away.

Becky jumped into her Subaru Forester that she had bought last year on a whim. She had wanted a family-friendly car but wondered if it was a waste of money. The car was great, but the reason behind spending a little bit extra had fallen flat. As she pulled out of the drive, she knew Carter wouldn't be happy with her.

She had been instructed to park in the underground parking garage at all times since the shooting had occurred earlier in the year, but she'd gotten back late after getting some shopping done at lunch. She parked in front because it took nearly five minutes to park in the garage, take the elevator, and walk the building length to her office.

She could redirect him with the overheard information and avoid the lecture for not parking where she was expected to. She had no idea what it meant, but she knew it was important information. What did Ramirez mean when he said he had ways to convince Jac to take the job? Shoot. Jac would be mad, and Carter would likely spank her, but she could say it was lucky she was there. Otherwise, they would never have known. Nah, that wouldn't work. They would both say she'd broken the rules. The men were so black and white sometimes.

She would shower, change clothes, grab something to eat, and head over to Ivy's. She'd help her set things up. Carter sent her a message and said he'd be a little later because he would stop and check in on a job they had just acquired.

Carter: Should I bring something home for dinner?

Becky: Not for me. I don't need anything. I'm going to Ivy's tonight.

The phone rang, and Becky rolled her eyes as she answered. "Carter. I'm running late. What do you need?"

"I thought we had discussed that you could go another time."

"Discussed but not decided. Ivy texted and said we were meeting tonight. Jessie won't feel like doing this for much longer."

"Rebecca..."

"Carter, I'm not a child. You don't want kids, remember? You can't Daddy me when you want to. When you make up your mind about us and our dynamic, let me know."

His low rumble sent shivers up her spine. She was so into this man and his dominant ways. She was doomed but a girl had to try to get her thinking through.

"You know better than that, and we will talk about this subject tonight because you will be home."

"Sorry, gotta go. We'll talk later this weekend if you like, but I can't stop now to hear the same old, tired song."

"Becky."

She cut him off. Her heart was pounding, and her bottom cheeks were clenched. She could feel her channel flood. He was trying to Daddy her by the sound of his voice. The man was such a gentle soul, but her cuddly man could change to a chastising grizzly bear and take charge of her in a heartbeat. If he would. Was he leaning that way now? Was he ready to resume their lifestyle? If so, defiance would put him over the edge.

Carter loved her. She knew that. The problem was he loved her but didn't want to share his deepest secrets with her. Time to find out why. This weekend, he said. She imagined she'd be sitting gingerly, but the conversation was necessary, and they needed it to move on.

Becky dressed for the weather that had stayed at a balmy thirty for the day and was now already twenty-six and dropping. She put on her extra warm boots and hat with matching scarf and gloves that Carter had bought her in four colors.

"I don't want to see you in this weather without them all on. Understood? It is a spanking offense."

There were many spanking offenses, and while they didn't seem to have bothered her before because she knew her Daddy loved her, they seemed to be pushing all her buttons right now. Still, she wasn't a stupid woman and staying warm was also her priority.

Her mom called just as she had put on her gloves.

"Mom, are you okay?"

"What, of course dear. I just wanted to check on you."

"Sorry but could I call you back? I am getting ready to go to a get-together. I'm running late."

"Well, if you are going alone, don't forget to get an Uber so you can enjoy yourself and have a few drinks. Let your hair down."

Becky laughed. "I was going to. Talk tomorrow, okay?"

"Okay, dear. Have a good time."

Becky had called an Uber before her mom had called but she liked someone on her side about it. She just needed a ride to Ivy's place about a mile away because she wanted to enjoy the night, not show up too tired to join in by walking it. She expected to drink so driving was not an option. And she was tired. Almost weary. What she wouldn't give for her and Carter to work this mess out and stop having these little snipes and disagreements. It was breaking down their relationship, and she hated it. She was sad most of the time.

"Expecting some snow later tonight," said the driver.

"Yes, so I hear."

"I might be back to pick you up, then."

"I doubt it. I usually have a ride from my friend's place. I just didn't want to drive in case I drank tonight. You know how it is."

"I do." He handed her his card since the trip had already been paid for online. "Just in case."

And they were there. She wouldn't tell anyone she called an Uber because Becky's long driveway seemed half as long as the mile to Kaden and Ivy's place. They would line up to take a swing at her ass for that. It was one of the things not allowed. Ever. Cabs either, for that matter. She liked that Carter had agreed on a house set back from the road. They'd chosen this house for privacy, and Becky decided she wanted it for the distance from the main road. Again, in the hope they would have children. Everything seemed to circle that one thing. It was hopeless. Ivy was standing at the door, waving her inside.

When Becky passed her, Ivy said, "I won't tell, but call me next time."

Such good friends.

Chapter 3

B ecky had already had a fancy drink and since she didn't drink much hard alcohol, it relaxed her. The drink relaxed her tongue as well. She told the girls some of the things that she was worried about. They had heard most of it before but as Becky seemed obsessed with the issue, she shared it again.

"I want marriage, but I also want kids, and you all know how hesitant Carter is to commit to that."

"Is he saying never?"

Becky's shoulders drooped. "No. But he isn't saying someday, either. I'm thirty-two, and my arms ache for a baby. It feels like my biological clock has been ticking louder these days. It's telling me I'm taking too long."

"I know it has to be hard when you want a baby, not to have one. For me, it's different," said Ivy. "I'm a long way from wanting more responsibility."

"I wish I didn't want one so badly. It would be much easier. Carter will do anything for me but this. I don't understand why he doesn't feel the same way I do. He loves kids."

Becky knew because she could see it in his eyes, and he was the most gentle, caring teddy bear she'd ever known. But sometimes she saw pain and that was confusing.

Sharlee listened before speaking. "So, it's the same story. What's stopping you from getting married is Carter doesn't want to agree to children. He says he isn't sure he wants them, but evidence points to another reason. So, I can only conclude that the way to solve this mystery and get on with your lives is to find the real barrier."

Callie rolled her eyes. "Just how much have you already had to drink, woman? That was stating the obvious."

"I'm tired of being brilliant. I'm on a brain pause." Everyone laughed.

"I spoke with Lisa, his sister, and as far as his family says, there is no reason why Carter should not be okay with kids. There was no incident or problem when he was growing up that they knew of that would make him hesitate to have kids of his own."

"I know it sounds bad, but I promise there has to be a reason that makes sense," said Sharlee.

It didn't make sense because he was so careful and loving. Becky didn't get it, and neither did their friends, but Becky focused on Sharlee's words and knew there was a good reason. She just needed to find it. The girls gave her some ideas and asked more questions between laughing and having too many sugary alcoholic drinks, except for the two pregnant ladies who drank virgins and peed a lot.

"What if you pushed him?" asked Jessie.

"You see if I do something that forces him to respond, then his true self stands up, and he pushes back just enough to stop me from doing what I'm doing. Unfortunately, the minute that happens, he realizes what he's done and backs up, literally and figuratively. I see the old bossy Carter that cared shine through, then he's gone. It's almost cruel."

"What if you just told him how you felt? You know, communicate?" asked Mallory.

"I have, and we have discussed it, but I don't want to hurt his feelings just because he might not love me enough to marry me and have a family with me."

"Don't say that. I can't believe that's true. You remember when Carter had girlfriends all the time... a different one every week sometimes, but when he decided he was interested in you, Becky, all that changed," said Sharlee.

Ivy said, "He gets very protective when you're around and when you aren't, I mean, he relaxes, but if there is a hint of anything happening around you, that man is an immediate tank ready to roll over anyone that even comes close to causing you any trouble."

The other women nodded, and it made Becky think she was making too much of things. "I know, but then he backs off. He doesn't carry it forward. It's like he thinks that the danger is gone now, so he can relax and let me do my thing."

"Don't you want to do your thing?" asked Jessie. "What I wouldn't give to do my own thing these last few months." There was a round of giggles.

"Yes, no... not always."

Callie nodded. "I get what you're saying, but Carter is a big guy. He can be scary. I've watched him want to pick up Storm, but he hesitates. If it wasn't that Storm is around a whole crowd of big, scary uncles, he might be afraid of Carter even though Carter is such a gentle giant."

Finley agreed. "I've seen it too. And now that you mention it, it's almost like he's afraid of something. Storm loves him and tries to climb him like a tree every time he sees him. But that might not be his perception."

"Do you think that's it? Do you think he is protective and has a few rules for safety and health, but he doesn't want to scare kids or me? Could he even think he could scare me after all these years of working and then being together?"

Callie shrugged. "It's just a guess. Why don't you ask him?"

"What you're doing now, guessing his whys and reasons is more harmful. If he's not meeting your expectations and you don't say anything, then it ends up breaking your relationship up. I think that's much worse than hurting his feelings. And if you want to know about the kid thing, don't guess; ask," said Mallory. She smiled. "Monroe would be bringing out his rubber paddle by now."

"No he wouldn't. You like it too much. He'd be bringing out his quirt."

Mallory shivered dramatically. "Evil device. Or worse yet, he'd make me write lines. I *hate* writing lines."

"Mallory's right," said Callie. "You need to be honest because, without honesty, there is no trust. You need that, or there's nothing solid that you're standing on. Learn from me."

"I haven't talked to Carter about anything important other than work in a long time."

"Don't you talk about your dreams, your hopes for the future?" asked Mallory.

"Sure, we used to all the time, but I see a future with children. Carter doesn't, or at least he isn't ready to share more than the surface things. Short term, you know. I'll have to think about how to bring up the subject and find out why he says he doesn't know about kids. But I expect another argument, or rather, he says he needs to leave, and I'm always stuck with my feelings."

Sharlee introduced a new subject after getting everyone fresh drinks. "It will work out, Becky. I have faith in you two. Now, I've got to say, these damn cards are driving Jac mad."

"Yep, if anyone wanted to get to Jac, that is the way to go," said Becky. "He hates puzzles." There was some time spent discussing where the cards came from and things that drove Jac crazy.

When it came time to go, Becky was going to walk home. She was close by, and if Carter was home, arriving in an Uber was a good way to start off on the wrong foot. She was glad they lived close to Kaden and Ivy, although their place didn't have a grand built-up property and house attached like Ivy's. But Ivy had a lot more family money than anyone else besides Jac.

The property itself was fairly large and was only about five miles from Jac. Garrett and Callie liked city living and would probably just stay in their nice condo until they decided if they were going to adopt a child or not.

Monroe and Mallory were in town, but they were considering moving closer to the country and the rest of them because Mallory was having their one-and-done baby. She was younger than Monroe, but since Monroe was staring at fifty, they would be more than content with one. Mark and Jessie lived about a mile on the other side of Jac and Sharlee in a house that was an ultra-modern smart home because Mark said he had no time or desire to fix a leaky faucet.

Carter's place, on the other hand, was an older farmhouse that Carter had made beautiful. He'd enhanced the already impressive character, and it was a showcase of his handiwork. Like his father and uncles, he had worked as a carpenter's helper, then full carpenter all the years leading up to and through college to pay his way. He enjoyed woodworking for relaxation, and the beautiful furniture he had made so far, were masterpieces. Many would say he was a master furniture maker, and their home showed off many of his creations.

Becky knew that it would cause an outrage if anyone suspected that she was going to walk home, so she slipped out while the rest of her friends were trying to organize themselves to leave. As she took off on the shoveled drive, she headed toward her house and wondered how smart of an idea it was because the cold began to seep into her bones the minute she turned into the frigid wind towards home.

Her gut tightened in uneasiness and a touch of unsettling dread. Regardless that Carter often said never to disregard your gut, Becky ignored her feelings and forged on. She fell into a chant of, "It's not very far. I can easily make it. No more exercise this weekend." The effect was less than optimal. She was still cold, still a long way away, and beginning to more than regret her choice as another gush of wind swirled around and past her.

Chapter 4

When you drive in a car, you don't notice the snow and cold the same as when you are on the ground, walking in it. It had obviously snowed and had been plowed in front of Ivy and Kaden's place. She thought about turning back when the plowed area faded behind her, and Becky found herself trudging through the snow-covered road, but she saw the lights to her house and figured she was halfway or more. Might as well get to her home rather than back to Ivy's.

The county removed the snow from the more elite houses first and then covered the less affluent areas. They sat smack in the middle, so sometimes they got plowed early, sometimes not. Carter said he was going to buy his own blade and hook it up to his work truck, meaning the truck he used to haul material for his projects. He'd begun to sell a few pieces to make room for creating more.

Becky had said he was grumpy these last weeks, but now, she wouldn't say anything again. This was getting difficult. She knew she should call Carter, and he was likely going to redden her butt however, it would be worth it. Wouldn't it? Except, the way he was taking a back seat to their lifestyle these days, rarely pushing the boundaries, maybe nothing but a scolding would happen. And he might not be home yet and didn't ever need to know. But she'd know.

A huge truck, much like Carter's, with running lights and big everything, was coming up the road with a plow in front of it. Where did it come from? His truck was around back the last time she saw it this morning. And it was covered in snow. Not that he couldn't have cleared it but was he likely to do that today? No.

It was kind of dark even with her LED flashlight that Carter made her carry everywhere. She could hear his words. "You need a flashlight. I know you have one on your phone, but you'll use up your cell battery for any distance when you could save it for calling."

Becky had argued with Carter when he went all bossy boyfriend on her, and when he didn't back down, she'd simply agreed. Now she was glad she did because the truck was leaving the road at the bend. As the truck drew near, the vehicle lights were almost overpowering. She hurried, using her flashlight, and prayed she didn't misstep. She waved the light and aimed into the cab, but it never slowed down. Finally, she was at the end of their drive.

The monster truck was about to pass her when it took a turn as though going into their drive at an angle. Becky yelled at the truck and waved her light at whoever was driving while she scrambled over the small bank. She slipped and fell into the ditch next to their long drive, unable to control the drop.

She hit the ground hard. She saw the cement drainage pipe just as her head hit it. Nausea, pain, cold, and fear assaulted her senses. Safety, was she safe? She couldn't think straight, and the darkness was surrounding her, adding to the rising panic.

Becky didn't know what the weight on her was, but her head pounded so strongly that she decided she must have hit it on the cement with immense force. Her body couldn't move. Her hands were close to her face as she tried to shield it from the freezing, wet snow being dumped on her. She was bent just enough to create a pocket of space between her and the snow below her. She kept her place, absently thinking it was an air pocket she could use if necessary.

There was no way to be sure, but it seemed that the truck was trying to dump more snow on her, purposely, but that thought was overrun by a fear that was nearly as smothering as the snow now covering her face and entire body. The panic was choking her. She couldn't breathe.

She could die here. She relaxed as the weight on her body became too heavy to support. She wished more than anything that Carter was there with her, helping her. He would know what to do and how to get to safety.

She could hear his voice in her head.

"Be still, baby girl. Breathe. Let your mind settle on the problem. What is the problem, Bec?"

"The problem? I can't breathe well. I'm cold. I can't move. I'm alone."

She tried to speak aloud, but she couldn't get her mouth to move. It was too cold, and there was too much snow.

"What is causing your problems?" her mind Carter asked.

"Snow. Snow is all over me."

"Okay, try to move some part of your body to get the snow away from you."

Becky tried. The world was deathly silent. It seemed even nature was holding its breath. Becky's head hurt so badly, and she was so very cold.

"I can't," she said to her mind Carter. *"You do it."*

"Rebecca Shea. You. Can. Do. It. Slowly move your body. What moves the most?"

"My hands. I can move my hands if I wiggle a little more. But it hurts to move."

"I know, Baby Bear, but do it anyway."

She thought about what a mean boyfriend he was because her head hurt and she was so tired, but his voice was so warm and inviting, she had to do it so she could cuddle in his arms. He would warm her up with his hot-natured body.

"I want a hot bath, and chocolate, and snuggles, and oh, it's coming out! My hand is coming out! If I can just... there!" The heat from her breath had cleared the area around her mouth, and she stuck her tongue out to touch the snow.

"No. Do not do that. Keep your mouth closed to hold in as much heat as you can, baby."

Becky pouted. *"I'm tired."*

"Don't stop now. You aren't done. Work your other hand out. You should have more room now. Get your face out of the snow."

"But I want to sleep, Daddy."

"I know, baby, but just a little bit more."

"I'm so cold."

"Becky, get out of that snow." He was yelling. Why was he yelling? Her Carter never yelled. Ever. He was a good Daddy. He cuddled and... Oh! I can breathe better. Cold. So cold.

Her hands were free, but her arms were still partly snowbound. She worked free enough to finish clearing the area around her face. Becky quit thinking and went on autopilot. She focused all her energy to get out. Exhausted, she got all but her legs out before she gave up the fight. She had her phone zipped inside her coat breast pocket, and she worked to get her fingers to wiggle free enough to unzip the pocket.

She looked around and, at first, was confused why she didn't see Carter. She was nauseous, and her head hurt so bad. She was stiff from the cold, and her exposed skin was numb. Even her gloved hands were numb. *Call Carter.*

She couldn't hold her fingers still enough at first to hit the number 1 key, which was Carter. Her gloves made it extra difficult, but she refused to take them off. Carter would be upset with her, and it wasn't a good idea since she was freezing already. Finally, after multiple fumbling tries, she got it. Pulling the phone to her ear, she listened to the ringing. Fear that he wouldn't answer cluttered her mind and crowded out her hopefulness.

"Becky! Thank God. Baby, where are you?"

"I... I'm in the s-snow at the end of our d-drive." She said, unable to say more.

"Okay, baby, I'm just down the road. I'm coming. Don't hang up."

She didn't answer but dropped her hand. She couldn't stand up out of the snow. *That's okay, Becky,* her mind told her. *Carter is coming. Just a couple of minutes.*

She saw several car lights on slow-moving SUVs, and a big truck, Carter's truck, pulled up and stopped.

The lights were so bright. "T-turn th-them offff," she rasped. They went to parking lights and big flashlights and people poured out of the vehicles but all she could focus on was Carter. He made it.

"WHAT BABY? TALK TO me. Becky, talk to me, hon."

Carter was back again. So cold. "C-cold."

"I know, hon. They have to warm you at a certain rate. But you will be feeling the warmth soon. Very soon." An enormous hand, probably Carter's, had wrapped hers up in his, but she didn't feel any more warmth. He was so hot-blooded; he was like a heater, so why couldn't she feel him?

What she wanted more than anything was to be warm and home in Carter's arms. There was something she needed to tell him. And Jac, but she couldn't remember what it was. Not even remotely. It would come to her later. And her head hurt. Becky's hand inched up in search of the pain and a hand almost too hot to bear grabbed hers and kissed it with almost too warm lips.

"You hit your head, baby girl. I know it must hurt, but you have to leave it alone. They stitched the worst of it but otherwise, haven't done anything yet. I think, once you are warm, they are doing a scan to see if everything is okay."

"I th-think this was on p-purpose. S-someone did th-this t-to me. They wanted to hurt me."

"No, baby. You just fell into the snowbank and hit your head. And got very cold, too cold."

"No. Listen t-to me." Several shivers ran through her body as the warmth from the blanket and the warm water he was given to ply her with did its job. There was also a warmed saline solution running by IV so the heated flush she could feel was in contrast to the cold she still felt. And she hurt so bad. Everything tingled, burned, and ached almost more than she could handle.

Jac and Sharlee knocked on the door. "How are we doing in here? You gave us a fright, Rebecca."

"I'm sorry, sir."

"Becky how are you feeling?" asked Sharlee.

"Better." Another shiver ran through her body as the warmth replaced the cold. But it also started her head to pound more. She moaned.

"She is in a lot of pain. Baby girl, is your head hurting more now? That's the warmth. I'm sorry, hon."

A nurse briskly entered the room. "Feeling warmer?" She didn't wait for a response. "Let's get you down for your scan and make sure all is well where you hit your head. Do you remember anything?"

Becky started to move her head, which elicited a groan. "No."

She wasn't sharing anything with them that was important. If she told them she thought that someone did it on purpose, and it wasn't just her falling into the ditch by accident, they would think she remembered wrong due to hitting her head. But she wouldn't change her mind. She knew it was done purposely.

"Well, it will come back. You're likely still in some shock. Okay, here we go." She had an aide with her, and they pushed the bed out with great efficiency. "We will return."

Carter paced as he waited for them to bring back his girl. He wasn't letting her out of his sight from now on. Shit, he just did. He turned to follow her, and a firm hand pushed against his shoulder. Garrett was standing in his way.

"I've got to follow them. I let them take her, and I can't let her out of my sight yet. I could have lost her."

"I'll walk with you. I know it seems as though you failed her. It isn't true, but it's where we alphas go in our heads, according to Callie. But honestly, that isn't the problem. Thinking we need to tighten things up is fine. The real trouble is when we begin to believe it was our fault, that we could have prevented things if we had only been there. Now that isn't sustainable, and we are more likely to lose our girl if we go down that road."

"Things are different between Becky and me. Our dynamic includes me taking over sometimes. I mean in every way. It's a stress reliever for her and, oddly, for me too."

Even as he thought it, he knew that wouldn't fly unless his girl needed it. She was a nurturer. She took care of everyone around her long before she examined her own needs. That's why he usually took over. She needed it but didn't say she did.

It ate him up inside that he couldn't share with her why he was so hesitant to have children. He wanted them with her. They would be so beautiful, and she would be the most incredible mom. That ability, however, didn't override his fear of what he knew would happen if he fathered children. It seemed like everything in their life circled around this one roadblock. Damn.

Jac and Sharlee had taken the information back to the others who were sitting in the waiting room. Garrett must have sensed that he needed that extra support. Odd, because it was usually Monroe, but now that Mallory had found out she was pregnant, even though she was still spending most mornings puking, he was less likely to leave her alone. Jessie was seven months now, and Mark had gone from stern and stoic to catering to her every need and smiling at inopportune moments.

Jac and Sharlee had decided to wait another year, and they were going to have their last child.

Sharlee had said, "We don't want Storm to be the only child. Kids lose that peer understanding that comes with a sibling bond if they are only children."

While not essential, both Jac and Sharlee were only children and wanted a sibling for their son. Kaden and Ivy were young and weren't sure they wanted that in their life. Children would take away from Ivy's carefree lifestyle. Kaden said he was fine either way. So, only time would tell how that played out. Mark and Jessie seemed content with one, for now anyway, and so did Monroe. Well, when they had their first.

Garrett spoke, interrupting Carter's inner musings while they sat in the chairs outside the radiology department. "Mark left Jessie with the housekeeper, but he's going home as soon as we're sure what the next move is. Jac is discussing it now."

"Where's Levi?"

"Still finishing up his assignment. It should be tomorrow. I think it's time we had a meeting about what Becky thinks actually happened."

"I don't want to say I don't believe it's true because she was adamant, but how could that be? A truck pushing the snow on her, purposely?" Carter rubbed the back of his neck. "I have a guy plow our drive, but he usually does it in the middle of the night or the middle of the afternoon."

Garrett gazed into the long hallway. "I don't know, man, but Becky is a straight shooter, and if she says that's what happened, I have to believe her."

"But who would do that?"

"No fucking idea."

"Yet," said Carter.

Becky rolled by and Carter grabbed her hand and walked with them back to the room. Garrett nodded and returned in the direction of the waiting room.

Chapter 5

Carter didn't want to think about the possibility that she had fabricated this whole thing or made herself vulnerable to arrive at this conclusion. What if he needed to give her more attention? Would she believe this happened because he hadn't acted like her Daddy? Her lover? Or worse, would she make this up to get his attention?

No, she wouldn't, and he hated that his mind went there, but he also had to acknowledge that he hadn't been giving her the Daddy attention she needed. He had been guilty of leaving her to her own devices rather than starting an argument or making her upset.

Time to change up his act, starting with rules. He would pull out her Daddy Dom until they figured out what happened and why. It was more than time, and she needed it. He needed it. He had to keep her safe; maybe it was time to make Daddy a permanent resident again. If she would even let him do more than the occasional dominant act.

He'd talk to Jac about how that would work at the office, but he had a clear vision of how things would change everywhere else. Damn, it felt good to flex himself again in the role that he lived for.

His girl needed him to take over and be her safe place. He hadn't pushed her because he'd been a coward. Worried about keeping the peace, but that was likely where he'd gone wrong. Becky was about to feel the heat of his demands of submission and earned consequences. Confidence flowed through his psyche. And he was about to face his own music. It was inevitable.

It was who they were, and he had been remiss. It was cruel to not ensure her needs were met when he agreed to be her Daddy. He wanted that role, meaning he had to man up and be that person again. They would deal with the things they had to deal with as they came up.

"She'll be fine. There isn't any bleeding or too much swelling and that has stabilized. No one needs to stay the night. Ms. Carrington is likely to sleep straight through. That includes you as well, Mr. Brackovich."

"I appreciate the thought, but that woman in there," he nodded toward the closed door of Becky's private hospital room, "she is everything to me. Leaving is not an option until she does."

The woman hesitated and said, "She's lucky to have you."

"It's the other way around, ma'am."

She regarded him for a few seconds and then stiffened her spine. "Right then. There is a makeshift bed, and I'll have someone bring you some bedding and a blanket." She put her hand up. "I know you guys are all ex-military and still hold the hard-ass award, but humor me and sleep on the cot. I'll check in tomorrow morning. If Ms. Carrington is doing well, I'll send you home."

"Thanks, Doc."

A deep, controlled voice spoke. "You good with staying here alone? I can leave Kaden or one of the others with you.

Not Mark. Even if he would stay, which he won't, he is a bear these days."

"Can't blame the man." Jac leaned his head to the side and regarded his friend and team member. "I'm good. Really. Thank everyone for us. We appreciate them showing how much they care. And before you all go, if you could grab me some food so I won't feel like I'm in some backwater place waiting for my relief, starving my ass off."

The chuckle Carter heard reminded him things would be all right. He and Becky had friends, knowledgeable friends who had skills. Lots of skills. And not one of them would hesitate to use those honed abilities to help when needed.

"We already thought of that. The girls have run off to get you fried chicken with all the fixings and whatever else they can find, including beverages. We need to discuss Rebecca, but we can do that in the morning. Even if they release her, it will be at noon. We know the drill. Call me when you know something new."

"Roger that."

"I think we have all been giving your girl too much power. She runs my office, hell, she runs me most of the time, but it is my office. The trouble, in this case, is Rebecca does it so well I don't mind letting her have her head. She knows when to rein in and ask permission, except she needs, craves the security of boundaries, accountability." Jac considered his friend. "By the look on your face, you have come to the same conclusion."

"I have. Things are going to be different now. Going back to the way things were."

"Glad to hear it."

Both men raised their heads as the women walked toward them with food in a large bag and a round, red and white cardboard container.

Carter grinned. "Girls, I could kiss you."

"Becky told us a while ago to quadruple your portion, so we did. Just take care of our Becky in there."

"Always."

Sharlee smiled at her husband, "We got our men food too. Didn't think you'd make it home."

Jac playfully swatted Sharlee's butt. "I taught you well."

"Well, me being hungry influenced you getting dinner." Jac grumbled but kissed her cheek before leading the group back to the waiting room to encourage them to go home.

THE NEXT MORNING BECKY woke up and discovered a weight on her arm. Panic was her first reaction until Carter's body moved when she tried to slip her numb limb from his grasp. She was still half asleep when there was pressure, like a kiss, on her hand as she batted her eyes in an effort to acclimatize them to wakefulness. The hiss from her as she felt the painful pins and needles sensation in her arm alerted Carter to her plight. Large, warm hands gently rubbed her skin, teasing the blood to flow freely through her limb.

Carter watched her for a moment. His baby was looking much better on paper than in reality. Her haunted look said she was far from recovered. The men had a short meeting from their homes earlier in the day to decide how to address things. He'd talk to her about that later.

He kissed her lips and stood to stretch. "How's my Baby Bear doing this morning?"

"I feel a little tired. My head is still pretty sore, and I have a little headache, but I'm good, really." She glanced at the garbage. "You slept here all night?"

Carter's anger brightened and yet deepened his Carolina blue eyes. Regardless of his facial expression, his voice was quietly intense.

"What kind of question is that? Of course, I stayed the night. I told you I wasn't leaving until you did." She'd heard him, but he could have left someone else to watch over her. She loved that he'd stayed. She did love him. It was just...

Becky shrugged as she watched his fingers plow through his dark blonde hair. Even though it was styled in a close cut, his top had been getting longer. She wondered if he had noticed it was thinning some on top. It made her smile. The next words were delivered with a firm but gentle tone. Becky's Teddy Bear evidently had a message to deliver.

"Rebecca, things are going to be different. It's been a while since I've been the man you needed, and while I've recently been lax about fulfilling my Daddy role. That ends now. Until further notice, you are under Daddy's watch."

Becky sighed. "We haven't done that in a long time. Not for more than a moment or two."

"And that's all on me. It's my job to take the strain off whenever possible and help to lower your stress, and I've not done that."

"But can you do that right now? I mean, we're all busy."

"No excuse. This is the dynamic we have, and that suits us the best. You are the most important thing in my life, sweetness, and with this recent event, until we find out what is going on, you are our prime concern. So, get used to it."

"But it can be so time-consuming and boring for you." She reached for his big, comforting hand and raised it to her lips. "You've done your best and I've been moody."

"Likely because you haven't been able to let go the way you want to. The way we both need you to. And you have run amuck without your Daddy to paddle or plug that backside when needed. So, as of now, you are doing as you're told. You are letting me carry the load, and when I get bossy, you will have two choices, use your safe word, or comply. I don't recommend any of your deflecting tactics or your circle-talking, my girl. Those will be met with sharp correction."

What could she say to that? Thank fuck would not be appreciated, and she would likely get her butt paddled before she even got home. She was so ready to give over that she would have shouted in relief, except it might bring the nurse in, and how embarrassing would that be?

She opened her mouth to ask a few clarification questions, and the door was knocked on and opened. The doctor smiled distractedly as she briskly entered the room.

"How are you feeling this morning, Ms. Carrington?"

"I'm fine. Can I go home?"

The doctor looked at Carter a little too long for Becky's liking. "So, can I go?"

Carter lifted his bushy brow as if to say, you go home when we say you do. Becky could feel her sex grow slick. She had no idea why this Carter floated her boat, but she had long accepted that about herself. Kink wasn't something she had ever thought of until Carter introduced her to who she was, and after that one night and day of passionate education, she was hooked. Right now, his chastising expression was making her belly jump and tingle. She wanted to climb him like a tree and build a treehouse in his arms.

"Ms. Carrington?"

"Oh, sorry. I was thinking about what I had to get done in the office."

It was a lie. Carter raised his eyebrow and tilted his head to the side as if to say, you want to stick with that story, little girl?

Becky ignored him and her belly. She listened as the doctor talked to her briefly after a quick exam.

"You look good. I'll let you go home after the nurse goes over the instructions. Your headache should go today or tomorrow, but no computers or electronic devices until the headache has been gone for at least 24 hours."

Carter looked skeptical. "Are you sure Doc? I mean, she doesn't look very good."

"It wouldn't do anyone any good to stay overnight again. And she is going to be sore, headachy, and bruised for a few days to weeks."

Becky opened her mouth, but Carter spoke quicker. "So, when her headache does clear, which should be a day or two at least, you want her off the devices at least another day?"

"Yep. Then she can go back to her regular activities slowly. Introduce one at a time to avoid any returning side effects. If the headache lasts for more than three days, come back here or get in to see her physician. Which I don't see on the paperwork. Who is that? I'll get it in the records."

"Um, it's been a while since I've gone in. I mean, I have my gynecologist, but..."

Carter's strong voice cut across hers.

"She can see my physician. Cairn Matthews."

Becky made the mistake of looking at Carter and seeing his mouth tighten. She knew what that meant. Thank goodness she had bits of concussion still needing care, or she had no doubt where she would have found herself, nightly, for the entire week.

Not seeing her physician regularly or at least annually was essential to catch things early. Carter had lectured her on it before, and she had assured him she was going. But really, who went every year when you were healthy? She avoided his stare. Becky knew she should have prioritized it, but she was still young. She knew that Carter, or even Jac in his work boss role, wouldn't be okay with her not getting a checkup once a year. If Becky remembered right, her last visit might have been when she contracted pneumonia at twenty-five. Yeah, not telling him that, either.

The hospitalist nodded. "Oh, I know Dr. Matthews. Nice guy. Good doctor. Okay, I also recommend you get in for an appointment with him. I won't ask how long, because I already know it's been too long. Now you have a reason to go. Do not forget to follow up if you have any complications."

The doctor nodded at her, allowing the physician to slide her gaze, with regret that he was taken, over Carter, who didn't seem to notice. Becky should have been pleased about that, but somehow, she wasn't as happy as she would have been if the female nurses and attendants weren't drooling over her man while standing in her presence. What was she saying? Becky didn't want any of them to devour him at any time. Great, now she was grumpy.

The ride home was difficult because the sun bothered her eyes and head, and she didn't have shades. "Put your scarf over your closed eyes. It'll help."

"I need to go to work."

Carter released a short, sharp "Huh."

"What? Jac pays me to work, not sit at home."

"Baby girl, you aren't returning to work today, it's Saturday. You're not going on Monday and maybe not until Wednesday."

Becky made a sound of outrage. Carter looked over quickly, spearing her with his intense chastising lift of the brow before concentrating on leaving the parking lot.

"Your Daddy has been letting you get away with too many things."

"Letting me?" came her insulted reply.

"Oh, yes. And that attitude had better hit the road. You won't be out of commission forever, and I intend on keeping score for your 'Come to Daddy' meeting."

She fell silent because she knew what he was saying, but the irritation, the frustration was building like a good head of steam with no place to go. Never a good thing.

"What are you thinking so hard about?"

Becky hadn't had him so attentive in the recent past, so hearing that while he was driving, eyes on the road, and still getting her vibes, was telling. It would not be a good thing for her in the short term. In the long term? Oh, yeah.

Pulling into their drive, she looked hard at where she had fallen, hit her head, and heard the big truck's diesel engine roar as it pushed that snow over her. Her breathing began to come in quick, shallow breaths. Her head pounded harder. Cold darkness seeped into her bones, and abject fear began to overtake her. She whimpered and moved inside her head. *Air, there wasn't any air!*

Warmth touched her arm, and she screamed. He was immediately crowding her, in her face, holding her hands. Breathing for her. Hot air rushed in. His voice was calm and warm, filling her, replacing the coldness that had burrowed deep with murmured words of comfort, whatever they were. More hot air. The touch and the sounds brought her back. His voice. Carter.

"You're with me, Baby Bear. You're okay. You're safe and secure in our house. Feel me, my breath, my hand. Smell my scent. Listen to my voice. You're safe, baby. I have you."

"Sorry," she whispered. "I-I don't know what happened."

"You were having a flashback if I were to guess. You've just gone through a trauma, and it will be a little time before you feel like your old self again."

"Like PTSD?"

"Yes, but you aren't likely to have post-traumatic stress disorder. Right now, you are having an acute reaction to trauma. We'll do our damnedest to make sure we address the fears head-on. I'll hook you up with our company therapist in Montana. Jocelyn is good at what she does. It will go away before it qualifies for a heavy diagnosis. We won't let it overtake you."

"Wait. I thought you were driving." Becky shivered as she tried to cast off the last vestiges of the traumatic memory.

His slow, devilish smile made every cell in her body take notice. "I've got skills." His smile was gentle. "I'd just pulled into the drive when I saw you were in your head and got you inside as soon as I could. Unfortunately, I only got to the garage before you needed me, but I wanted to be available to support you or just wait it out. When you start falling into your memory try to pay attention to things around you. Jocelyn will help with that. It might have been why..."

"I'm sorry," she whispered.

Carter's face flashed irritation and then it was gone. His demeanor gentled again. "None of that. The rule against saying bad things about my girl includes apologizing when it isn't your fault. It wasn't your fault so you can't say sorry. Okay, let's get you out of the cold and into clean, warm pajamas."

His arms slid under her thighs to the back of her knees. He scooped her up in his arms and the strength and warmth of his body went a long way toward soothing her fear-heightened nerves. He'd done it countless times before they were struggling with the marriage question. The baby question.

What did he mean that it "might have been why?" Why what? That might have been why she had the fall and the snow dumped on her. Because she was in her head? That she thought it was intentional. Another mystery that needed to be addressed.

"It wasn't an accident. It was deliberately done. If you have doubts, I will stay somewhere else."

She tried to be as adamant as possible, but her mind was screaming to be careful not to blow this relationship like the others. In previous, less long-term relationships, she'd demanded acceptance of her ideology and agreement with her thoughts of how life should be. It had been the beginning of the end of the two relationships she'd had worth sticking around for and they were nothing like this one.

She was sustained by this relationship. Her thoughts were screaming in painful fear that was stronger than the physical discomfort her headache was causing, Becky needed to know that Carter believed her. It was important. She needed to know he was on her side and trusted her thinking.

He looked into her eyes, studying her. "No, but I wondered, at first, if it was because you were in your head that you missed the signs. But you're right, that's not logical given the facts. There are too many loose ends, why would someone dump the snow in a drainage ditch in front of the house? And why had no other houses had their snow plowed? Why did it stop plowing after this house? Because it was obvious that is what happened. No, baby, I know something isn't right here."

Becky shivered. "Thank you for believing me."

"Bec, I'll always believe you. Come on, we have to get inside. You're getting chilled." Before she could remind Carter that she could walk, he slid his other arm to her back, tightened his hold, and lifted her.

"My bag." She didn't carry a purse so much as a bag she used for a purse.

"I'll grab it after I get you on the sofa. And if you argue, I'll swat that behind, regardless of the headache. Got me? I'm taking care of my Baby Bear."

She did get it. Carter was shifting into Daddy mode—hard, and she could feel herself slide into what she called her pampered headspace. She leaned in to smell his Daddy scent which was different from his Carter scent. She couldn't explain it, but Daddy smelled like heated leather and warm spice. Carter smelled like energy, man musk, and sizzled.

Daddy was comfortable, and Carter was strength. When Daddy was home, he had a quiet authority that no one would question, but gave you that feeling of seclusion, safety, and home. Carter was muscle and power. He manipulated the world around him to secure her.

Daddy was stern, a rule-maker, an enforcer. And he was her disciplinarian, which included spankings for naughty and fun times. Carter was denied orgasms, extended teases, and spankings, because when he kissed her, suckled her, cherished her, she was loved. And both experiences were hers in one man. Women who wanted two men just wanted one Carter.

Becky knew to sit when those emotions evoked by his dominance filled her as few other things did. Strength flowed through his words, wrapping around her like a warm, weighted blanket. His attention to detail was meticulous in all areas of his life, but when it pertained to her, it felt as though he directed all his attention on her, for her comfort, her protection. She belonged to him, as she would never belong to another soul, and if Becky allowed herself to dwell on the significance of it all, she might drown in the fears of the insignificant. The thought that something could happen to him, and she would no longer have him could bring her to tears. But she was normally a look-on-the-bright side kind of person so it was not someplace she would go when he held her in his arms.

"Rebecca Shea, pay attention to Daddy." Becky turned to connect with her lover, eye to eye, and nodded but wasn't sure if she'd missed something important.

"Reach into my pocket and grab my keys."

She reached into his front pocket, and her hand felt around until it nudged his penis, thoroughly aroused. She lifted her eyebrow and giggled.

"Oh, my. Um... do you need me to take care of something for you, Sir?"

"No, and my back pocket, baby. My dick can wait until you're well, and then you will take care of things. It's been a while since I've had you where I wanted you."

Becky nodded because she knew she'd avoided sex with him these last weeks. She missed it too.

"And you wanted me to look where exactly?"

"Pay attention, baby. Grab the keys and unlock the door, little girl, before I toss you over my shoulder and do it myself. I don't think your head would handle that too well."

While she hurried to get the keys and unlock the door, she spoke jokingly, "You could carry me around instead of lifting weights."

She laughed. He greeted her with a Machiavellian look giving her a tremor of anticipation of what he had in store for her when she was feeling better. Even though he hadn't slept well last night while in her hospital room, Carter was making sure that she had everything she needed. He should have been grumpy, but he wasn't.

"I could carry you if you like, but I wouldn't get enough of a workout."

"Or too much of one," Becky murmured.

Putting her feet on the floor, he closed and locked the door. "That's ten, Baby Bear, payable when you are well again."

"Hey, what was that for?"

"Think about it; I'm sure you will figure it out. I'll help you if you haven't answered your question by the time I've finished my phone calls and made us some lunch."

"Oh, I can make lunch." A sharp pain shot through her bottom cheek. "Okay, I won't then. I'll sit in the living room."

"Good. While you still can. How about in the recliner unless you want me to put you to bed?"

She shook her head and hissed. "No, I've had enough time in bed, thanks. I'll just sit in the recliner."

"Good plan. I'll bring you a blanket and pillow in case you get tired."

Instead of arguing she wasn't tired, Becky let him fuss. She loved it. She had already pushed a button unintentionally by referring to herself as overweight. Becky didn't usually miss that, but the thoughts crept back occasionally and tripped her up. Shoot, she really was feeling tired. Likely the effect of the pain medication they gave her for her headache and body aches. But the actual ache was deep in her core. Carter in charge was a sight to behold. Becky sighed deeply, a contented and submissive sound as if all the world's worries had been washed away.

"Hey, baby, you need to eat something." The clatter of their lunch items set down on the coffee table brought her awake, but she was groggy.

"Sleepy? Do you want to eat later?"

Carter's voice was like a warm summer breeze flowing over her still bruised senses, comforting Becky in ways she could only feel and making her needy bits even more hungry for him.

"No, I'm hungry, I'm just in a fog."

With Carter's help, she scooched herself to sit against the pillow and pulled up her blanket, wrapping it around her, drawing on its comfort. It's security. It was a poor substitute for being in Carter's arms but then she looked at him, wondering if he was going to just pick her up because she could see he had an agenda.

"You okay like that?" Becky nodded. He put his lip on the edge of the soup spoon before lifting it to her mouth. "Good. We have things to discuss."

Chapter 6

Carter watched his girl's expression as the emotions attached to her thoughts flitted across her face. It was a good thing that she didn't play poker because she would never win. And that's just how he wanted her, open, honest, and genuine. Sometimes though, it got in the way of protecting her, like now.

Becky needed more than she had ever shared, and that probably came from her growing up in a family and environment with a more stoic outlook on life. When you're faced with an obstacle, you have two options: face it head-on regardless of the effects on yourself or turn away and ignore its existence. For Carter, neither of those things would work, and it had taken a while before he and Becky had come to an understanding.

If it was something that Becky did not want to manage herself, that's when she handed it off to Carter, but under no circumstances was she to ever ignore a problem because it only got bigger. And the bigger it got, the more unwieldy it became. His girl had found herself over his lap many times while learning that concept, but he thought she eventually got it because she came to him more often now.

The newest situation with Becky, however, showed that wasn't always the case. She knew something or thought something or misunderstood something, and it had become a problem, and instead of coming to him, she had ignored it. He didn't know what that was exactly, but he had no intention of her hiding it any longer. It was time to take over.

He fed her a few more bites before speaking again. "We need to talk about things. Set some ground rules."

"Carter..." Her heavy sigh communicated the rest of her sentence.

"Rebecca Shea, you will hear me out. I'm speaking as your lover and your Dom."

"I get that I scared you, and you weren't there to stop bad things from happening to me. I get that it rubs you the wrong way when you think things might be out of your control, but I'm careful, and putting more rules in place won't help."

Carter could feel his stomach muscles clench. He needed to clarify before he headed in the wrong direction. "Are you saying our dynamic no longer works for you?"

"No. I love who we are. I love you taking over when I need it, but it can't be because I had an accident."

"So are you saying the incident was not deliberate because it was a different story earlier."

"Honestly, I believe it was a deliberate act but maybe done randomly. The thing is, if I treat it as an accident, I can deal with things better. If I don't, I might be scared out of my mind."

Her sentence ended in a whisper, and Carter had to hold himself back, but it was almost impossible. He knew they wouldn't get it all out if he gave in and cuddled before they were done.

"If you think it was no accident, then I have no choice but to go on that. I'm sorry if you would rather forget this mess ever happened, but I can't. I don't know what I would do without you. If you were hurt on my watch, I would never recover if I lost you," Carter took a deep, shaky breath. "Hell, even knowing you are safe and sound right in front of me gives me heart palpitations when I think of last night. "

Carter had to touch her more than he currently was with his hand on her extended leg. Standing, he arranged the lunch closer to the end of the sofa and scooped her up from the recliner and relocated them to the sofa. He never wanted to put her down or stop touching her. But she was hurt, so doing more than taking care of her immediate needs would have to wait until she felt better. But it didn't mean he couldn't cuddle her.

Becky squealed, and Carter automatically smiled. He loved that sound, and he usually heard it with his head between her thighs, feasting on her pink bits.

"Daddy, you didn't warn me."

"I love it when you call me Daddy. It fills me up."

Becky smiled sweetly. "I know. It makes me happy too."

"I think we need to lay a few things on the table here. I'm confused, and you could straighten me out."

She plopped back in his arms and sighed heavily as her look of resignation said so much. "Fine. What is it?"

"You're a Little or you'd like to be."

"I am not. I've never said that."

He nodded in agreement. "Right, you haven't, but you have said that you want a man that takes the reins and handles the heavy stuff, so you don't have to."

"Okay." Becky's agreement held caution in her tone. "But that doesn't mean I'm a Little. Lots of grown women want that. I don't want to go to a different age in my head. I just want to be taken care of at my own age."

"Right. So, when I said that I was taking over, in previous times, you were good with that, it fit your needs, and you have even asked for that a few times when I didn't do it quickly enough." She nodded. "And you like to watch the younger movies—"

"And lots of others."

"Yes, okay. But when we watch action movies, you close your eyes and sometimes cover your ears."

"So." Becky scrunched her face as though she was trying to make sense of what he was saying, but Carter watched her begin to fidget.

"So, you at least have Little tendencies. That means you like when I take over, you even crave it."

"Not all the time."

Carter kept his smile locked down tight. "No, not all the time, but you do want there to be rules, boundaries, and guidelines, and me to enforce those. It's what you have been missing since I have backed away and lived the vanilla lifestyle with you. I've missed it too."

Becky didn't say anything, but her thighs squeezed together tightly. "That's what I call my pampered headspace because you are pampering me. Every woman likes pampering. And your point is?"

"My point, Little girl, is that you have pretty strong tendencies, and you want those things I do for you. You want me to be your Dom, so you don't get to pick and choose when that is. Your safety and all health concerns come under the Daddy heading, and I intend to do my best to meet those responsibilities. I made a mistake by letting other things get in the way, but

I've learned my lesson, and that little hiatus is the only one we will have."

Carter resettled Becky in his lap with both of them extending their legs on the sofa, her peanut butter and honey sandwich in her hand, having finished her soup. He kissed the top of her head.

"I'm sorry about the rules, baby, but I have to know you are safe."

"I know, but I'm careful already."

"Baby, this isn't because you aren't. I have to make provisions for whoever did this last night. Like watching out for the other drivers because they are an unknown entity, not because you don't drive well."

"I get it. But I'm not a Little. I just like when you Daddy me... mostly."

She reached for her cup of milk, and Carter passed it over. It had a sippy cup top, so he didn't worry about her dropping it on herself. She was tired. Becky wasn't one to drink out of cups designated for adult Littles, but she enjoyed the water bottles you sucked from the top. He liked that she liked them.

"I'm too old for a sippy cup. How embarrassing."

"You're never too old, and this is a regular-sized cup. I like that I don't worry about you spilling on accident. Saves you, me, and the sofa. It's really just like the water bottle you use at work."

"I know, but it's a water bottle that millions use, not a big cup with a sippy lid."

"Duly noted. I'll grab a couple more sippy water bottles."

"You don't want to let me win on this, do you?" she asked wryly.

Carter smiled. "Not when it's the same thing, and you are doing what you always do when I'm trying to set down rules, you find a way to make your passive-aggressive side win. It is like your sippy cup, but you want to be the boss, so you want to drink from the water bottle, but the same mechanism is in place." His voice deepened to get his point across. "Don't make this a habit, or I'll take full control."

"Like?"

"I'll hold the cup while you drink from it. Or I could be even more controlling."

"No, nope, I'm good. I'd love to drink from the sippy water bottles. Absolutely delighted to." She sucked on the tip of the lid as though it was just fine with her.

Carter chuckled. "Good choice." He patted her thigh. "But there's more. I don't want you to be alone. Not in the house, not coming or going to work, not in the store, yoga, nowhere."

"What? No, that won't work. Carter, I have a life and work. I enjoy being alone sometimes. I need it to recharge."

"Hear me out. It isn't as bad as it sounds."

"No, it's worse than it sounds. I have to put a limit on some things."

Becky started getting up and screeched when he landed a sharp slap on her thigh, partially exposed from under the blanket. She squealed her outrage at the sting his hand left.

"No. You will not misbehave while Daddy is talking. Listen to it all, and then you decide if it is something to argue about."

"But you always win, and I don't want you to win this time."

He turned her head to place a soft kiss on her lips, then hugged her close to his chest. "I can't allow you to put yourself in danger until I'm sure I've neutralized any threat. So, this is how it will go. I will talk to Jac, but I'll be your bodyguard and driver when needed. If you go to yoga, I'm sure you could go with Ivy or Mallory. They'll have no trouble doing that. I'll pick you up."

"Oh, you mean I don't have to have a goon with me everywhere I go?"

"Goon? I'll let the guys know their new title." He kissed her cheek and laid his on the crown of her head. "You mean too much to me to compromise on this. I'll still sit outside or in the lobby, but it will allow you to get some girl time in. Also, I'll be the one at home. If I can't be, for some reason, you will have to take another guy. I'll try to keep the choices from the Alpha team, but I can't guarantee it."

"But my alone time."

"Baby, I'll leave you alone as much as I can... as much as you want, up to a point. I still want my baby in my bed, cuddling with me on the sofa, having dinner with me. None of that will change. It's just your trips out of the house and office that will be accompanied."

"Okay. I guess that isn't too bad. But who goes to the grocery store?"

"You order, and we will pick it up, or I'll have them deliver it."

Becky smiled. "Good, because I hate going shopping."

Carter rubbed her chilled arms and tried to cover her, but she pushed it away. Right now, he had to pick his battles. This wasn't one of them.

"I know. See, some good comes from this."

Another sigh. "Fine, I guess. But I reserve the right to re-negotiate."

Carter was glad she couldn't easily see his face. His grin of victory would have turned into a grimace of a discontent. He took a break to eat his sandwich. Carter didn't mind that the bread was drying out. He dipped it in his lukewarm tomato soup and was just thankful to have his girl with him.

After a moment, Becky asked, "Um, are you on Daddy duty?"

He swallowed his bite. "Yep. You will not disobey me, and I have the last say. New subject. You've been working on your dad's paperwork to help him, and it's frustrating you."

"It is, really. I can't figure out this crazy inventory number. Dad doesn't carry much backstock; if it's Uncle Karl's, he must label it like that. And it's too much besides. I'm going to have to go there pretty soon to figure this out."

"Sure, we can go as soon as I can get a break."

"What? You hardly ever go. My dad isn't very kind to you."

"I know why, but if I'm not discussing marriage with you, I'm certainly not discussing it with him."

"I know. But we are going to need a conversation again."

"Sweet love, as soon as this is resolved, I'll have that conversation with you. And I promise we will settle it."

She nodded. "Okay."

He polished off his sandwich and left the cold soup. Stacking her chicken noodle soup bowl under his, Carter began again.

"Now, on to the next issue at hand. You left Kaden and Ivy's place after drinking and walked to the house, in the dark, on the side of the road. What do you think Daddy is going to say about that?"

Becky turned and snuggled into Carter. "I just didn't want to be a bother."

"Not the right answer, baby. You are never a bother to any of our friends. But that isn't news to you, so you'll need to do better than that."

"I'm sorry. It was a dumb thing to do, but I wasn't thinking clearly, and not because I had a few drinks. I thought I could get there quickly."

"Rebecca Shea..."

"Fine, not entirely because of that. I had thought walking in the brisk air would sober me up so I wouldn't be all headachy and moody when you finally got home. And then you wouldn't ask me how much I'd drank, and I wouldn't have to tell you."

"Is that the only reason?"

"And I was irritated with you because you didn't follow me out of the office when I left from work."

"I regret that. It won't be happening again. Another reason why you didn't call me for a pick up. So, tell me now. How much did you drink?" His voice had deepened, and he felt her shiver. Good place for her mind to be, under her Dom's control. He encouraged her. "Go on."

"I don't remember." Carter could hear the quality of her voice change.

He hardened his tone. "Tell me what you remember. Be honest here."

"Um, I remember four or five."

"Which means you probably had more. Don't we have a rule that if we are not together, you can only have three unless you are staying over?"

"But I was with the girls."

"Yep, and you should have let someone take you home. So, that whole fiasco costs you ten."

"Fine."

"For a week."

Becky gasped in surprise. "What? No way."

Carter continued with a pained look in his eye as he remembered the night before. "Baby Bear, when no one at Kaden's could find you, they called me. Luckily I was on my way to pick you up anyway, so I was here quickly. We were all looking for you. They'd checked the house but could easily see no one was home. So, they began to walk the area, starting from Kaden's place toward our house when your call came through. They'd already passed you."

Carter took a moment to stave off the fear that had overcome him when he thought something terrible had happened to her followed by the realization that something had. As it was, she could have frozen to death or suffocated in the snowbank. He could have lost her. It wasn't something he could think about for long, or he'd wrap her up in bubble wrap, in a padded safe room when he wasn't around to personally protect her.

"There are going to be consequences for that little drama. Not the accident but the trying to walk home in the first place, which allowed everything else to happen."

"Are you saying it was my fault?" asked an annoyed Becky.

Carter ran his hands through his hair and took a deep breath. If this was going to work, honesty in communication and a strong reality check would be in order. He chose his words carefully.

"I'm saying if you intend to be reckless with my baby, there are going to be some consequences that you might not expect but should. You could have died. The person most important in my life would have been gone due to her choices. That is unacceptable. I love you. You say you love me and if that is true, you will do all you can to protect that love by being safe."

Becky's soft sniffles could be heard. He kissed the top of her head again. He loved this woman more than life itself, but the lesson had to be learned well.

"Don't you think you deserve to feel Daddy's hand on your bottom? Spanking you hard so you know I love you and don't want anything to happen to you? To remind you that whenever you want to do something unsafe, you will remember the heat of your little backside as you felt the sting of my hand landing on your ass cheeks for seven straight days to remind you? I'll hold your hands fast so there is no covering. Your control will be gone. Then Daddy will slap your bottom hard, leaving his handprint to remind you that I love you and you are precious to me. And that you are never to put yourself in danger again."

He could feel her ass cheeks twitching and thought the expectation would be worse than the spanking, so he'd let her sit with that vision until the headache was gone for good. The anticipation would be an incredibly horrible pre-consequence mind fuck.

And a huge sexual turn on. The moan told him she was aroused now with just a little erotic talk about what he would do to her. He could keep that up throughout the next few days. He wouldn't take her until that headache was gone, either, so she would be as miserable or more, as if he were edging her. She would be so needy by the time they got down to business, she would be butter in his hand. Yeah, by the time her punishment actually happened, she'd be begging him to spank her. Maybe he was a little sadistic at heart.

Time to put his girl down for a nap. She was tired and the guys would be coming over later this afternoon, to see what they could piece together of the incident. She needed to be rested. Her headache was better, but the more she rested, the better it would be. He'd dropped the ball in their relationship, but he was determined to pick it back up.

Later that afternoon, after Becky got up from her nap, Jac and the guys all came over to discuss what Becky knew or didn't know and to try to solve this mystery. Their closest neighbors were Kaden and Ivy, and they watched their video during the event.

Kaden pointed out several big personal trucks driving past during that short block of time. "Becky, you're sure it was a POV?"

"Diesel. I remember the sound was huge, and the truck was huge but not a snow truck, more like one of those monster trucks. Like Carter's truck."

Kaden ran the video until it came to the time frame she was on the road, and then he slowed it down. "Any of these?"

As each truck passed, she shook her head. Then one showed on the monitor, and Becky yelled. "Stop. Stop. That's it. That big white truck. See, it has a snow blade on front."

Kaden began tapping on his tablet. Sharlee, online with her big computer brain at home, started clicking her keys, and soon images began to appear on one of the triple set of computer monitors that Carter had in his home office. It could be over-whelming at times, but, like Jac, his office was large, his computer was massive, and, of course, the monitors had to match.

As images of trucks, videos, and screenshots of information began appearing, Carter moved them from one screen to an-other until each monitor held a different data set.

"Rebecca," said Jac, "are you able to identify any of these ve-hicles?"

Carter hid his grin. Jac was back to referring to her by her full name. It had taken several years to train him to try Becky, but the name didn't work for him. The man just wasn't going to use any name but Rebecca. Rolling her eyes, Becky concentrat-ed on the trucks.

Sharlee spoke on the video connection. "Try to envision what they would look like from your position as a walker and then in the ditch after hitting the culvert."

Carter cringed. They didn't know that Becky had already had the beginnings of a panic attack when they drove past the spot earlier. Reliving things from the position she was in when it happened could bring on another. He opened his mouth to speak but Becky spoke first.

Becky shook her head, "Other than big, white, and diesel with a plow, I don't know. Sorry."

Carter shook his head. "Nothing to be sorry about."

Sharlee sighed. "Thanks, but it means you can't identify the right truck or person."

"It looked like a truck I'm familiar with, similar to Carter's but different. I'm still trying to work out where I've seen it before," said Becky.

Carter kissed the top of her head. "You'll remember."

"I hope so. So now what?"

"Now we start working on a plan to keep you safe and figure out what's going on here," said Jac.

"You're not going to stop me from going to work. Because Jac, if you think I'm just going to stay home and let people figure things out, you've got another think coming. I've got lots of projects going, and there are meetings to set up, papers to file, a new employee to set up with orientation, and a whole lot more. I don't just sit around eating bonbons, you know."

At first, Jac didn't say anything. He just focused his calm, intense stare on Becky. After working with Jac almost since the business started, Becky knew exactly what that meant. Jac was either humoring her, waiting for her to stick her foot in her mouth or engage in other self-sabotaging moves. Her boss would be quiet and look like he was giving you all your due respect. Which a person couldn't deny he was doing, but it had a purpose: to let you run out of steam before he gave you the final plan by laying down the law.

It wasn't a plan he was suggesting but a strategy to be executed without question, and today Becky would need more time to agree to that. So, she thought she'd get all her words in first because once Jac spoke, it wouldn't matter how many words she used. They wouldn't change his mind.

"Carter and I have already discussed the things that have to happen to keep me safe, and I'm on board with it. But if you're going to say that I can't go anywhere or drive myself or any other super restrictive things, I call foul. You guys don't even necessarily believe that it was on purpose." Becky looked around the room and crossed her arms from her seated position. "I've seen how you guys cut your eyes to each other or look away when I said it was not an accident but let me submit some information you may not know about because you weren't privy to it. First, since we've been here, no plow has ever pushed snow in the ditch in front of our house. We pay for snow removal, and no one else on the road after Ivy and Kaden's place had been plowed. Like always, they wait until the snow has stopped or in the middle of the night. Midnight is not the middle of the night. And we did not pay for immediate removal which isn't what happened anyway."

"Becky, I absolutely believe you, but if I'm being honest, I can't say that I noticed very often where the snow was pushed when they cleared the roads. But all the rest, absolutely true."

Carter wasn't being mean. He was his typical trustworthy self, and she couldn't fault him for that, although it did irritate her a little that this was the time he chose to be totally transparent instead of when she wanted to know why children were such a significant roadblock for him.

"Oh, and my scarf was very bright. You guys have seen my knitted scarf, hat, and mittens sets. You've all commented on them at one time or another that I was like a neon sign entering a room. I had those on, so to say that he couldn't see me in the dark was ridiculous. It would have been obvious the minute lights hit my head.

"Or when my flashlight shined in the air and all around me trying to get his attention. But despite the fact that I was so bright, the truck and the plow continued to come off the road in my direction."

"She's got some excellent points," stated Mark.

"And finally, I'm not one of those drama people. I'm the person who tends to assess everything in front of her and then decide. I have thought about this and am positive it wasn't an accident. I don't know why or if I was some random victim that some crazy person saw and decided to share his lunacy with, or if I was targeted or was a target just at that moment, I can't say. But I can say if you guys don't believe in me, then I just want to let the police figure it out."

Carter went down on his haunches in front of Becky's chair and grabbed her hands while staring into her eyes. She looked down.

"Sweetheart, show me your eyes. That's my girl. I'm going to speak for everyone, and they can take it up with me if they have a different opinion, but we do believe you. We have to look at this clinically because if we don't, we let our emotions get in the way we feel because it's one of ours. It will cloud our judgment causing us to miss something significant. So, bear with us while we get through this. Okay?" Becky nodded her head. "Words, baby."

"I do understand. It just feels like I'm out here on a limb, dangling without a net."

The room was quiet for a few moments, and then Jac spoke.

"Rebecca, believing you is never a question. The question is do we have enough information to do anything about this incident? If this is all the information we have, then there really is nowhere else for us to go except to try to troll things like trucks that went by during that time frame on other cameras and back track. We can modify it with additional descriptions that you come up with as you remember things. There are no distinguishing items on the truck, and we didn't get a shot to enhance the license plate. It's going to be tough if not impossible."

"I know."

"We intend to return to where you had your accident, but I don't think we'll find anything after so many people have been tromping around out there. But we're still looking. So that leaves us with only one other option to keep you safe, and that's to put in more restrictive safeguards than you're used to. You know we can get much worse if something else happens. The lockdown safehouse is the final response when we go hunting."

"Jac, have you talked with Carter about the things I agreed to do? It's enough."

Jac moved to replace Carter in front of Becky. He, too, went down on his haunches to lessen his appearance of control. He clasped his hands together and leaned his forearms on his thighs. Becky wondered, not for the first time, how these big men could hold that position.

"I have. And I only have one thing to add: if you hear anything or remember anything or know anything, you have to promise to tell us."

Becky nodded. "Jac, I might have overheard something important. Even if it's not important to what happened to me, it might be important to you."

Jac patted Becky's hand and said, "Okay, tell me what you know."

Becky thought that Jac would stand up and walk away but he didn't, he stayed right where he was, and the only thing Becky could think of at that exact moment was his knees were gonna hurt. If it weren't so serious, she would have giggled. Becky proceeded to explain what she had overheard in the car.

"I'm being very clear about not knowing the context. I don't really know what they were talking about. I just know what it sounded like, and it sounded like they were talking about you Jac, because he did use your name once. I also know Ramirez stared at me pretty hard before telling his driver to drive away."

Jac seemed to contemplate for a moment, then patted her hands one more time before standing and briskly walking over to where the monitors were. He started moving things around on the smart board, throwing out some information and leaving some still on display except in a different position. He looked at Kaden.

"I need you to screenshot these and shoot them to Sharlee. Carter, you're on Rebecca duty until further notice. Garrett, can you do more digging and find out what we don't already know about Ramirez? Concentrate on his recent dealings. And get Callie to check her sources for this period since she signed the contract with me two days ago. She's on my clock now, so it's time to get her feet wet."

Garrett murmured something about making his life harder. Jac just smiled and pointed at the board again. "When they're all pulled together, send the info to Sharlee for compilation. Levi will be on another unrelated job for a few days. Kaden, just for tomorrow, I need you to hit the local safe houses and make sure they're stocked and have everything that they need."

Jac looked around the room. "We're going to meet for a few minutes every day to debrief on this issue but unfortunately, it isn't the only one we have on our books and so you'll have to do your part in between new assignments as of tomorrow." Jac turned to Becky and said with all sincerity, "We will figure this out and, in the meantime, if you stick with the plan, we will keep you safe. And if you don't…"

"I get it. That means I can go back to work?"

"Carter?"

"She has to be 24 hours without a headache and that won't be until at least Monday, maybe Tuesday, but then she can go back to work if she's feeling up to it."

"Rebecca, Carter is my new gauge as to whether working is good for you or not. So, if he says you can work, then you can work. But if Carter says you need something or something is too much for you, there will be no question from me. If I have to, I'll ban you from the office. So don't push me, sweetheart. Understood?"

Becky opened her mouth to assert her ability to know whether she was fit to work, but at Jac's look and then Carter's face of warning, she sighed.

"Understood."

Chapter 7

A week after the snowplow incident, nothing seemed to happen, and the guys thought they could add a few more jobs to their plate because they had nothing to go on. There were no new leads, no new incidents, nothing.

After another week, Carter went back to work on other assignments away from home. The team discussed and agreed they would return to normal operations except for Becky, who still had a couple of restrictions that, according to Jac and Carter, were "just to be safe."

Becky was allowed some freedom, like driving home, well, to Ivy and Kaden's house until Carter arrived home. It had meant one overnight at Ivy's because Carter had an overnight job, but she could handle that if it ensured that soon Carter would allow her to resume normal operations.

EARLIER IN THE MONTH, Becky had found some paperwork that didn't seem right. Inventory numbers seemed excessive for the amount of storage space. Now, after reworking things she was still just as confused as ever. She'd mentioned it to her dad at the beginning of the month but now she was ready to tackle the problem.

"Dad, I can't see how this is possible. I mean, look at your numbers from when you started the business. Remember when you filled the place with inventory, which was entirely too much, so you had to rent additional storage until you sold enough backstock?"

"I'd forgotten that. Kids remember everything. I remember the time you—"

"Dad. Listen. I have a three-day weekend coming up. Why don't I come and re-run the numbers for you? I can't run the inventory, but I can recheck most of it and do a better estimate. If it is close, I'll accept the packaging of things is less, so you can hold more." *It would have to be considerably less, but she'd keep that info to herself for now.*

"Should I tell your uncle to do anything?"

"No, just tell your warehouse manager I'll be there in a few days."

"You got it, sweetheart. Is your beau coming?"

"Carter, Dad. His name is Carter. I think he's on the job."

"What does he do again? He can't make much money as a security guard. Big guy like that, a pilot and ex-military? He should be able to get one of those high-tech, flashy, security team jobs. You know, like mercenaries or something."

She bit her tongue. If her father knew that on a high-profile client, Carter could make ten grand in a weekend, she knew her father's new favorite hobby would be to get them married quickly.

"He does pretty well, actually."

"Well, I'm sure your income helps."

Carter paid for everything except some food and the personal items she snuck in. He wanted to pay for the things she bought, but a girl had to pay her way somehow. Yes, it fattened their savings account, and this summer would pay for a swimming pool if she could commission it and pay for it before he caught on.

"I hate that you're wasting part of your weekend to verify that Monty made a mistake, but your mother will be glad to see you."

"I'm excited to see you too."

THAT EVENING, AS BECKY and Carter were having dinner, Asian takeout, she found she was still thinking about the inventory.

"Don't you like your dinner? It's your last takeout this week, so you had better enjoy it. I said I'd cook dinner tonight."

"You did, but I never know when you're coming home on these types of assignments, and I didn't want to cook. I was hungry."

"This is the last time, get me? If you pick up fast food before next weekend, there will be consequences."

"But I like variety."

"I do too, but you have had egg rolls and orange chicken tonight, burger and fries another night, and you brought home pasta on Monday. No veggies on any of these choices. I'm putting my foot down. A bunch of empty calories with little nutritional value."

You can't afford to gain weight, is what she heard. *You're too fat.* She knew Carter was just kind and not saying what he thought aloud, but she could hear it in her head. Suddenly, her enjoyment was gone. Everything lost its taste. Becky put down her egg roll and wiped her hands on her napkin before putting it on her plate. After taking a moment to swallow her hurt, she used her hands to push off the table to stand, and even that embarrassed her. I can't *even stand without help.*

I will not cry. I will not cry. Not in front of Carter, anyway. As she entered the kitchen, big fat tears heated her cheeks as they rolled down to drip off her chin. She scrapped her plate in the garbage disposal before placing her plate in the dishwasher, she leaned on the sink and tried to control the flow. Just as she lost the fight, she felt powerful arms wrap her tight, signaling her push to hide from the only man she had ever truly loved, defeated.

His deep, warm voice sent painful longing through her body. "Come on, baby, let me hold you. I need to comfort you." Once she turned to bury her face in his shirt, the dam wall, supported by her willpower, burst, and the flood of tears quickly made the front of his shirt soggy.

He picked her up, and the thoughts running through her mind unchecked ran out of her mouth without one filter operational.

"I'm sorry I'm too heavy," she said as she tried to escape his arms.

He stood stock still. "I thought that was it. Rebecca Shea, Daddy is going to spank you so hard. You know that isn't true. You also know I was talking about nutrition, not calories, body size, or any other nasty things your brain is trying to tell you. I owe you anyway for the same thing when we came home from the hospital. For not loving my baby the way I do, unconditionally. You know what I think?"

"No."

He chuckled. "Too bad. What I think is you have been working on your dad's paperwork a lot lately and that brings you to think about home, your parents, and your mom and sister who always made little side comments about your weight."

He might be on to something, but it still hurt. She started a fresh round of crying and felt his soothing touch as he rubbed her back. Nonsensical things were coming out of his mouth. It was what he did to ease her. The sound of his voice and the feel of his protective arms around her gave Becky the comfort she longed for.

Finally, after sitting in his lap for a while, she'd cried all the tears. Hiccupping on occasion, Carter patted her back one last time, held her away from his shirt, and ended her hiding.

"We have talked about this, haven't we? Your body image. I could have had my pick if I had wanted a woman with tiny boobs and no butt. I love your curves, spankable ass, and more than a handful of breasts. It feels like you are a real woman, not a paper doll. I'm a big man, honey and I don't care what you look like. If you're happy, I'm more than happy because I love your curves. But if you lost a little weight or gained weight, I'd still love you, want you, desire you. You'd still be mine."

"But my tummy isn't nearly as flat as it used to be and nothing like Callie's. My hip bones aren't protruding like Ivy's."

"Really? Now don't get me wrong, I love Ivy like a sister, but she doesn't have anything I want in body style. She's great for Kaden, but for me, I need to cuddle with something soft."

"But soft means squishy."

"And that's bad because...?"

She sighed. "I'm not a stuffed bear and I don't look good in a bathing suit."

"That turquoise number you wore last time we were at Jac's was hot. I jumped in the pool to hide my erection because my trunks sure weren't doing it."

"Oh."

"Yeah, oh. Now you owe me twenty for that and the last little comment about your weight and me carrying you. Then I never made you pay for the ten swats for seven days you owed me for taking off from Kaden's at night."

"You can't give me thirty in one night?"

"You've done more when we were playing. But I think it's important that I do all thirty. Baby, I am very lenient with you, but I don't think that's what you need, is it? I think I had this all wrong. You need a strong lover to spank your ass, cuddle you close, and tell you hell no, when needed. It's how we used to be, and then, when we had that conversation about marriage and children, I backed off."

Becky nodded. "I know. That's when you quit being my Dom in a real sense. I thought it might have been me. You didn't want to be with me or that dynamic anymore."

"That is all wrong and it's my fault. I wasn't secure enough in our relationship to push that envelope and tell you anything else, so I hedged and hid. I demand honesty from you, yet I allowed my fears to separate us when it was important to be open. That's all on me. I made a big mistake, and I'm so sorry."

Becky plucked at his flannel shirt buttons. "I think you're right. It was then that I had trouble connecting. I felt disappointed when I pushed back hard against you exerting your position, and when you didn't hold the line, it felt like I didn't matter as much, or you didn't want to be with me anymore. It hurt."

Carter held her tight. "I know, and I felt that was the problem, but after I started down that road, I wasn't sure you would be okay with changing things back. I needed to face my fears, then conquer them. But it all starts with you."

Becky leaned back and looked into his earnest, vulnerable eyes. "I do want things to go back to where they were. I've missed my Daddy, and I've missed my Carter. I've missed it all," she said in a near whisper.

"Then that's where we go. Start back at the beginning. We'll go slow and ease into it if you like."

"Carter, I don't need to ease back into it. I miss our dynamic so much. I miss *living* it. We refer to the lifestyle and dance around it, but I want it to be real again, not when things get crazy but every day."

Carter was quiet as he examined Becky to see if it was truly what she wanted. No saying yes when she didn't mean it. He saw only openness in her expression and hope.

He cleared his throat and nodded. "Good enough. Let's start as we mean to go. Our rules are back in place with the extra ones rescinded, except being more careful of your surroundings. If anything changes, if you feel off, or that something is not quite right, you must tell me immediately."

"Within reason." Carter's brows raised, and Becky clarified. "I mean if I can't get through to you because you are on a high-stakes assignment."

"Then you'd be at someone's house, not staying here alone. You know the roster and who to call first. I think you created it. The team has decided that is how we will do things from now on. Our women don't stay alone if we are on a VIP assignment."

"Carter, that isn't necessary."

"Yes, it is, and it's how we're doing this. No arguments, or there will be consequences."

"Is it too late to change my answer?"

"Yep. We're doing this." He kissed her lips hard and thoroughly.

Becky sighed and spoke in a low voice, "Yes, we are."

Carter dropped another kiss on her lips and put her on her feet. "Time to pay the piper, baby. Drop your panties."

"But my head hurts now."

A slow smile spread across Carter's face. He ran his thumb over Becky's lips, and she sent her tongue to meet it, circling, sucking on the tip, staring into his eyes. Her eyes were dark with arousal.

"You are one sexy woman, Rebecca Shea Carrington, and headaches are truly bothersome. Crying will do that to you, but now I think we need to get the punishment over, so you only have one tear-induced headache to deal with instead of another one later."

"I don't think this relationship is fair."

Carter chuckled. "Okay, so what do you think should happen to make this fair? Spankings every day for a month to balance things out?"

"No, that isn't what I mean. What I mean is when I make a mistake and choose to do the wrong thing, I get punished, but when you make a choice that you know is the wrong thing, you get no punishment."

"Like what?"

"Like when you avoided the situation and backed away from me when we discussed marriage. You left me emotionally adrift. You always talk about honesty, yet you weren't open and honest and still aren't. That is a punishable offense."

"Fair enough. So, what do you want as penance?"

"I want to... um... damn it. I get a chance to turn the tables, and I can't do anything. It's just not the way we do things in our relationship. I don't want to be the one who chastises."

Carter smiled. "Okay, how about this? After I spank you for your unfortunate choices, I'll come clean about why I have reservations about children, and we can talk it out while you eat ice cream."

"Rocky Road? It has nuts and those are healthy."

Carter cringed at the sugar in that one. He was thinking more natural strawberry or vanilla, but a deal was a deal. He nodded. "Rocky Road it is."

"Yes! With chocolate syrup?"

"Don't push it." He kissed her. "Now, panties off. You have ten seconds."

Becky hesitated momentarily, but when his fitness watch came up so he could time her, Becky kicked into action and pulled off her tights and panties under her flowing skirt. Carter loved spanking her when he had to lift her billowing skirts. He patted his knee and moved his hands to allow her to settle over his thigh.

When she was in place, Carter tossed her clothing up and patted her bottom, circling, kneading her cheeks, warming the area so his swats wouldn't bruise. Her skin was light, and her coloring came quickly under his hand. He loved that look and the increasing sounds of discomfort she mumbled. It made him as hard as it made her wet. Yeah, they were made for each other.

At the beginning of their dating, her quick skin coloring had worried him the first few times that she was over his knee, but soon, it was apparent that coloring or squeals were not good indicators of anything but light skin and rising libido. Spanking was an art form with rules and precision he was sure Becky didn't consciously appreciate, but in the practical application, he was sure she did.

Carter was forever grateful that his girl allowed them to share this in their relationship. It fed his Daddy Dom's need to pamper, protect and correct, but it was also sexy as fuck. He punished in other ways, which also worked, but when he spanked, he rarely ended the experience without his girl getting a spectacular orgasm. Tonight would be no exception.

Becky's beautiful backside was warm and medium pink. Just how Carter wanted it. She was utterly relaxed. Yep, that looked about right.

Chapter 8

Carter's hands caressed her bare bottom as he began to spank her, and the sensation made her gasp with the suddenness of it. The sound of flesh meeting flesh filled the room as he brought his hand down hard against her naked, quivering bottom. With each spank, she felt a thrill go through her body as she imagined her skin beginning to turn from pink to red. Her breathing became labored, and Carter ignoring the sound of her pleas for mercy only made her more aroused. This was the man she had lost for a while. He was back in full form, and she sunk into the emotional rush of his control.

She could identify the scent of her own arousal, which was thick in the air mingling with the heightened maleness of his essence. The feeling of Carter's firm hand rhythmically bouncing off of her lower cheeks was like a drug, lulling her into the pleasurable pain she ached for. She needed more.

"More," she begged, arching her back to present her now flaming backside to him.

The tears were close, but she didn't want to simply cry. She needed more. Becky's mind and body demanded that she wash away all the trouble and mistakes she had made lately. The pain of Carter's rejection still hurt, and she wanted all of those misunderstandings cleansed away.

"Becky baby, are you sure?"

"Yes, I need it. Please," she begged again.

"Use your word if you need to."

His hand landed harder and harder. Her desire coursed through her veins, and she was determined to feel every bit of her passion and guilt, his disappointment and fear, and their need. Becky couldn't get that final release of culpability otherwise. She'd almost died for her recklessness. As she rocked on his thighs in desperation, vainly chasing that release of her guilt, she gasped and wailed in defeat.

"No, I can't... I need..."

"I know what you need, baby. Hold on."

He moved her slightly away from him, and she collapsed in devastation. He wasn't going to finish the retribution she needed to pay. She reached over to bite his calf to bring on the finish she needed until she heard it. The rattling of his belt buckle and the swooshing filled the room and echoed back. Her belly trembled at the familiar, telltale sound that told Becky he knew his girl and loved her so much he wouldn't allow her to sit in her unresolved guilt. That he understood she had almost ruined it all.

He placed her on the sofa. "Kneel up, Rebecca." She scrambled into place almost too eager for someone about to feel the lash of her lover's leather. "That's Daddy's good girl. Now lean over the back of the sofa, bottom presented."

She did. The anticipation was debilitating, causing a tremor and antsiness she knew Carter would not allow for long.

Carter's presence was commanding, from the firm grip of his hands to the way his shoulders squared when he entered a room or declared his decisions. His voice was a gentle rumble that vibrated through Becky's core, making her feel at ease and safe even when he was about to exact punishment. She melted when her Daddy dominated her, when he drove her to places of brilliance that she had never been without him, when he opened views into her very soul and exposed parts of her she'd never known existed.

Under his protection, Becky melted into his embrace, his muscular arms around her, keeping her safe and secure even when over the top, like recently. Carter's voice held an underlying authority that sent shivers down Becky's spine whenever he spoke. She sank into his words like a warm embrace.

His voice wasn't cold, but it was made of steel. He brought with him possessive protection. Firm, assertive, decisive, secure protection. Becky knew Carter didn't like to punish this intensely. He was a lover first, but Becky had always needed cleansing when things went wrong due to her actions. She was a person who needed to atone, and Carter saw that. He offered that cleansing, forcing it on her even when she initially resisted. He knew her so well.

No other words were spoken as the belt flamed her ass. It drew a deep groan from the depths of her core. Yes, this is what she needed. Two, three, four swipes of the leather across the plumpness of her bottom. The fifth landed across the tender sit spot she'd known he would address. He always did when using his belt. It achieved the goal more quickly. She expected it every time and yet was surprised when he landed there. Then six, seven on her upper thighs. Yes, just a little more. The pain was almost too much. She almost safeworded in defeat but then three final leather stripes, delivered in the exact same spot, her tender transitional sit spot. She broke.

Carter stopped. He sagged over her and kissed her flaming backside. His sigh was loud when he kissed and fondled her almost desperately. She cried hard as his tongue found her small brown entrance that he teased before moving to the throbbing entrance to her inner wetness. He needed this as much as she did. Carter leaned over and ran his short nails over her throbbing scorched bottom, searing it again. She cried out in erotic pain.

"Don't move," he said sternly.

The thrill of this Carter nearly overtook her. She ached and hurt and was so damn stimulated by the spanking, his belting, then hands, lips, and tongue attending to her needs she almost didn't breathe. She could feel the warmth radiating off her partner's body as he moved his hands down her body, sending shivers through her with each gentle caress. The atmosphere was thick with expectation and the scent of their combined arousal. He got rougher.

She let out a low moan as his touch became more insistent, his tongue more intrusive, and the sensations grew more intense. She closed her eyes, focusing on the feeling of pleasure that was building up inside her. The sound of her partner's breathing grew heavier with each passing moment, and the smell of their arousal now filled the room. She pushed back against his mouth, and he slapped her outer thigh.

"Don't be naughty right when I'm about to fuck you. I'm taking your sopping pink entrance, and you'll let me. I'm not going to be gentle about it, baby. This is part of your punishment for putting yourself in danger and almost dying. For ignoring our rules. How could you still think my baby isn't perfect for me? That she won't always be perfect for me?"

He thrust his cock in hard and fast, taking her breath away. Her throbbing body's response was, "Yes!"

He was taking what he wanted from her, and Becky was desperate to give it to him. He pounded into her roughly, his fingers biting into the flesh at her hips. Finally, as the waves of pleasure peaked, she cried out in sheer ecstasy as she experienced the long-awaited orgasm that mixed with her tears. Beautiful release. That last piece of the puzzle that said his disappointment was gone; his love was all that was left. She was free of regret and guilt. All was right in her world again.

One climax rolled into another as she peaked and just as she succumbed to the tranquil peace, another wave rose and overtook her. Somewhere in the harsh beauty, she heard his roar of release and he slammed into her almost violently, taking what he wanted, and she was left to exist in the shattered bits of her fireworks. It was breathtaking, brilliant, exhaustingly destructive, and healing.

They lay on the wide couch as they caught their breath and snuggled. This was a required activity, according to Carter. Becky had never had sex as she had with Carter, nor had she experienced such a complete cleansing as Carter could give her. She'd never felt as whole as when she had connected with this man. But now it was his turn. They dozed for a while as Carter idly played with her nipples and kissed her gently in the interludes of sleep. Finally, Becky spoke.

"It's your turn," she said.

"You don't forget things when it's something you want," chuckled Carter.

She wiggled and hissed as her backside rubbed against the leather material on the sofa. Without a word, Carter pulled her up on his belly, and he arranged himself to be comfy as she wiggled on his partially aroused cock.

"Woman, we have had enough for right now, and if your backside isn't tender enough, you are in a good position for me to help that out."

"No, no, I'm good. Sorry. But it's your turn to clear the air."

Carter sighed. He patted her bottom, feather-light. She hissed anyway. He smiled as she knew he would. It was their dynamic, and it fed her soul.

"Okay, so I told you I didn't want kids, and that wasn't the whole truth. I do want them, but what I didn't know, or at least hadn't admitted to myself, was that I'm afraid to have children."

When Carter said nothing more for a few minutes, Becky raised her head from his chest and looked into his eyes. His vulnerability was easily seen, and that told her what she needed to see. He didn't have to say anymore if he didn't want to, but she hoped he did. The painful inevitability of his agony over this subject pierced her heart. And hurting Carter was never something she wanted to do. But she took a breath and slowly let it out as she waited.

Not allowing him to purge this from his system and clear the air was an injustice for both of them, and she wouldn't do that. Just as the spanking cleared the debt she felt she owed their relationship and had swept away the guilt, he needed this to go on. This didn't need to stand in the way of their happiness. He had the power to break the bond this had over him, over them.

"Take your time." She kissed his chest. "I love you."

Carter rubbed her back and kissed the top of her head. "I'm sure you've noticed that I'm a big man. Adults seem to be able to deal with that pretty well but children, not as much. I can't tell you how often I've encountered small children or even older ones who hid behind their parents or screamed when they looked up and I was standing there. Even when I sat down on the floor with them, they did not want to interact with me. I frightened them. I don't want to frighten my own children. It would destroy me."

"It never dawned on me that your size would frighten children, but I had begun to wonder if it were something like that. To know you is to love you, honey. You're so gentle and kind. Kids would love you if they could get to know you. I'm sorry that has been your experience, but I can guarantee that our children will never be intimidated by you, scared of you, or any of those other things you have experienced. You'll be their father. No one will be more representative of safety and comfort than you."

"You will have the market cornered on comfort."

"Maybe, but you are who they will expect to protect them, play with them, be their security in life and their big teddy bear. You are all they will have ever known. They won't know anything about what other people think or that you're too tall, big, or anything else. All they will know is you are theirs."

"I hadn't thought that if I was with them from the beginning, they wouldn't have any concerns. I'd be normal to them. Hell, what was I thinking of waiting and pushing you away?"

"You thought that it would break your heart if that happened. And you figured it was always going to happen. But if you had trusted me with your secrets, I would have been able to help you think them through. And a side effect of having children who think you are just perfect as their dad is the other children who know them will also think that. They will follow your children's lead."

Carter seemed to digest her words as Becky slipped her hand up his tee shirt and rested her hands on his hot skin, feeling the hills and valleys of his muscled belly.

"Storm doesn't have any trouble with me, but I just figured it was because he was used to me, and all the men in his life were big."

"That might be because he has known you since he was born. You're one of his people."

"How did you get so smart?" asked Carter.

Becky lifted her head from his chest and grinned. "Some people are just born lucky."

A playful slap landed on her sore backside. She squealed and then moaned. "And some smart people have no common sense. I guess this is the time to tell you I didn't wear a condom when I took you tonight. You are still on your birth control, right?"

Becky paused and then shrugged. "I am. I should be okay. Maybe."

"Get up, baby."

She pouted. "Why?"

"Because we have a ring to buy. I'm not risking it."

She laughed loudly. "Don't be silly. Besides, the store is closed by this time on Saturday. But we *can* order takeout for supper."

"No more takeout. I'll make us breakfast for dinner later."

"Pancakes?"

"Becky, pancakes aren't very healthy. Ham and eggs."

"But I've had a hard day," she said with a pout.

"I guess you have, and you've been a good girl. Blueberry whole wheat pancakes and ham it is."

"Yay! With Rocky Road ice cream on top."

"What? No, absolutely not."

"You promised me Rocky Road ice cream."

"No more desserts this week."

"That's not fair. I can't help it if you promised me something and then forgot and promised me something else too."

He quickly scooped her up, his long legs eating the distance between the living room and the kitchen. "Then you had better eat all the healthy parts first. I'm throwing in some walnuts with the blueberries."

"Fine." He popped her backside lightly and quirked his brow when she looked up at him indignantly. "Sorry. That will be wonderful, Daddy."

"I thought so." He dropped a kiss on her nose and sat her on a stool at the kitchen bar. She squeaked and hopped off, rubbing her afflicted bottom. She looked up just in time to see Carter's grin as he turned to the refrigerator. Meanie. She loved him so much.

Chapter 9

Jac had brought Becky in on the last strategy meetings on what they had found out concerning her accident, and this time was no different. Carter thought it was bringing up things that he wanted her to forget, but when Jac had offered Becky to sit in on the meeting, she had accepted. Usually, Becky would only sit in on specific meetings if Jac needed her. He could record the conversation, and the technology was covered by Kaden and Sharlee.

Jac was a man with many irons in the fire, and it was up to him to oversee every team and keep up with clients he cultivated or that found him. Those that he said weren't too much of a pain in his ass. Becky realized that even with the less desirable businessmen or women, if they didn't ask him to do something he was morally against and they paid well enough, he found someone willing to do the task.

The men that aligned themselves with Jacquard & Associates did so because they believed in what they did and if they had a personal issue with something, they could bow out. They had done many things in their earlier careers that they had no say about and didn't always agree with. Their leaders were not always upstanding citizens and sometimes let power go to their heads.

Jac didn't put up with that shit. If he got that feedback from someone, he watched and had Garrett and others watch. If they verified the issue, the person in question was out on his ear whether he was operative or client. Callie and Sharlee were the only women on the teams, and Jac tried to keep them out of the line of fire. Callie didn't like that very much, but Jac had explained that Garrett would have his ass on a platter and then bury the rest of him alive if he put Callie where they knew there would likely be active gunfire or danger.

Callie paced the room. "Jac, that's sexist."

"No, that's the rule. We have already discussed this before you signed on the dotted line. If you have a problem with it, go to Garrett, and if he clears you for that kind of active danger, then he can assign you to those jobs. I won't. And if you think you can slide in when no one is looking, ask Sharlee how that worked out for her."

Garrett had quickly cleared up any misunderstanding about the cases she was welcome to be in on and where that line was drawn. There were a select few she wasn't to be considered for, but the rest were open season for all but Sharlee. Becky agreed that these guys were too protective sometimes, but when needed, she knew the women were glad for it.

Waiting until Jac was ready to go into the conference room set aside for Carter's team, she let her thoughts move to her father and the inventory discrepancies. Tax time would be soon, so she knew it needed to be correct to report to the accountant. She had gone down and spent the day and night with her parents, but it was obvious she was going to have to do something else.

Her father thought that his brother's inventory had been mixed in by mistake or that the two business' paperwork was confused somehow. Suddenly, it was no big deal to her father, but it still didn't make sense to Becky. Why now, after years of never having this happen? She'd figure it out this weekend and then encourage her father to retire.

His memory was getting spotty, and he seemed much more gullible than he had even been a year ago. The story is that the warehouse manager might be at fault. Too much work, not enough workers. Putting the issue aside until she could visit her parents and discuss it with her dad, Becky followed Jac into the conference room.

Becky sat on the left side of Jac, which was her usual spot in the meetings, with Sharlee on his right. Carter sat next to Becky. Garrett typically sat at the other end of the table, with Callie next to him. Since most of the guys had significant others now, they filled in, leaving space for any wife or girlfriend who might have needed to be part of a meeting.

Mallory never came to a business meeting, stating she liked her work but was considering sitting on the board. She'd chosen not to return to the pharmacy where she'd been kidnapped from, not once but twice. Now working as a distance pharmacist where no one knew or saw her was perfect. She would follow up on medications mailed out to customers to ensure they didn't need help understanding the side effects or had questions about their prescriptions.

Ivy was doing a brisk business in her martial arts studio, and Jessie was the head numbers cruncher for Jacquard & Associates. Right now, accounting wasn't her biggest worry. It was her unbending husband, Mark, during this pregnancy. Becky sighed wistfully.

She felt Carter lean over to whisper in her ear, "Bec, you okay?"

"I am. Sorry about that. Just thinking."

"Okay, Rebecca, let's get your business out of the way and then we can go onto last week's recap of finished assignments and this week's jobs to decide from." Jac looked directly at her. His voice was precise but gentle. "We have done as much background work as we can, and while he is a royal asshole, there is no indication that Ramirez is the reason for your snow escapade. We found he was somewhere else at the time of the accident, and his top goons were with him. It doesn't mean he couldn't have done it, but he consistently uses his trusted few for most jobs."

"Okay, so who was it?" asked Becky.

"And that is a question I don't know if we will ever answer," said Garrett.

Sharlee nodded. "It seems likely that it was a random act of aggression not targeting you but choosing you out of convenience of place and time."

"So, I was at the right place at the wrong time."

Monroe shook his head. "No, young lady. You were in the wrong place at the wrong time. I'm sure Carter has expressed disappointment in finding you on the road, alone, after dark, in the cold, having imbibed several drinks beforehand."

Becky wiggled at the memory and nodded. "He has. I'm sorry for diverting you from going home just to deal with me and my stu-issue."

Monroe nodded. "Thank you, but your issue, as you put it, could have ended in your death. You are much more important to us than getting home on time. However, don't do anything that risky again, or whether Carter takes care of you or not, I'm bringing out my rubber paddle."

Carter laughed. "I might have to borrow that sometime."

Becky blushed because while others thought it was a scare tactic, she knew it was because she might like it. Best keep some secrets between her and Carter.

Jac continued. "What I'm saying is stay alert, but all indications are it isn't something more nefarious than it appears."

Becky nodded. It made more sense that it was an intentional accident. If she was a victim, by chance, she could handle that. She leveled a stern look at the alphas in the room. "Okay, so all following me around is done with. I am returning to business as usual but will be more cautious."

Mark, the most serious of the bunch, said, "And use the phone when you need anything."

"Yeah, or Sharlee will make you use her tracking program."

The room nodded as though in agreement. "That is an excellent idea," said Sharlee.

"No, I'm fine. You know I never could get that thing to work right."

Carter leaned over and whispered in her ear. "That would mean more freedom for you, little girl. Or, you can have me keep underworked associates continuing to follow you."

"I'll talk to Sharlee later."

"Good girl," said Carter. And she was aroused and needed clean panties. Just. Like. That.

The weekend was quiet. Her parents had something going on so a trip home this weekend was out. Becky asked Sharlee if she and Jac would go out to dinner or something so she could bring Carter over to watch Storm.

"Pick a day when Finley is going out with either Ryker or Levi."

"Sure, but why?"

"I want to prove to Carter that all kids aren't afraid of him and that he'd make a great dad."

"Did the contract Mallory gave you not work?"

"I didn't use it. I wanted to make sure that I understood Carter's reasoning, and after he finally told me, I figured I could prove to him that he was wrong. We talked and worked a lot of things out. Storm is an easy kid and is familiar with both of us. I thought pushing Carter over the line with proof might be the way."

"Okay, did he agree to it?"

"Well, he agreed that he loves Storm, and that Storm isn't afraid of him. Does that count?"

"No, but it's good enough. I want it known though, that if you get in hot water over this, remember I did not encourage you. I just went on a date with my husband."

"Absolutely."

That night, Becky and Carter arrived at Jac and Sharlee's with dinner ingredients in hand.

"Tell me again why we're here?" asked Carter.

"Sharlee wanted a nice dinner, and when Florent is gone, no one can cook adult food past steak and potatoes. She said Jac wanted something decent, so Sharlee asked me what I made since I cook more than any of the ladies, except maybe Mallory."

"And what did you tell her?"

"Shrimp Scampi with steamed veggies is one of your favorite meals. So here we are, having Shrimp Scampi for dinner. Go see if you can find a tasty wine. I'll get things started in the kitchen."

Finley came out of the downstairs nursery and handed Storm over to Becky. The adorable child lit up with a smile and immediately began babbling when Becky started talking to him. "Put him down around eight in his upstairs crib. I have his routine written down. See you later."

"Thanks. Bye."

Becky was walking into the living room as Carter came up from the cellar. "I pulled out a nice bottle but not an expensive one. If Jac wants to change it, he can."

"It's Finley's day off. She just handed little Storm off to me on her way out. Um, not sure where the other two are. Here, I can't take Storm into the kitchen while I'm cooking, so could you take him?"

Carter looked at his little girl and squinted. "Am I going to be itching to spank a beautiful bottom tonight?"

"For fun, maybe? But not for serious. Absolutely not."

Dinner took half an hour to finish. She'd already prepped the veggies knowing that if she fed Carter quickly, he would be happier.

Table set, Carter walked into the dining room and handed Storm over to her. She also had the little man's dinner ready and sat him in the high chair. Storm immediately reached for

Carter. She tried to distract him with food, but he wanted Carter.

She made a face. "He doesn't want me. Maybe you can get him to eat his dinner."

Carter hesitated before taking the spoon and grinning at Storm, who watched the utensil leave the compartmented plate and move toward his eager mouth. Carter spoke to the little boy, his voice low, but said nothing to Becky. She was slightly concerned, but at least her point had been made. Carter was great with kids; if they knew him early, there was no hesitation to cling to him.

Dinner was made, and Becky helped entertain Storm while they ate dinner. Carter spoke to the little one and talked about his upcoming week but not a word about what had happened here.

When it was time to put Storm to bed, Carter helped Becky get the little boy to sleep. Carter sat in the rocker next to Storm's crib, and soon the little man was asleep. Carter got up, checking the monitor before he left and grabbing the extra speaker on the side table before closing the door behind him. Special operations pilot's training came in handy when you needed to use your stealth to steal a plane or exit a sleeping child's room.

As Becky started the dishwasher, Carter walked in and firmly sat the baby monitor on the counter.

"Rebecca Shea, you and I are going to have a stern talk about lying to your Daddy."

"Oh!" Her hand flew to her chest. "Don't sneak up on me like that. And I didn't lie."

"You said Sharlee and Jac were going to be home."

Becky shook her head. "No, I didn't say that. I said she was asking about something good for dinner, and I told her what you liked."

"Then why did we eat that for dinner, which was done perfectly as always, but at Jac and Sharlee's house."

"Because they went out to eat somewhere."

"I asked you where they were."

"And I said I didn't know because I don't know where they went. And before you ask, it is Finley's day off, and she is on a date with Ryker. I think she has a date with Levi tomorrow. Not sure what he's doing, but she's playing with fire."

"Yes, it does sound like it, but she might have learned that from her friend, who will soon apologize for misleading her man while looking at the ceiling."

She scrunched up her face. "The ceiling?" Then the realization hit. "Oh, no! You are not spanking me, and definitely not that way."

"Daddy's choice when it's for punishment."

Becky's shoulders slumped. "I only wanted to show you that you will be a great dad, and children love you. I was stunned when Storm didn't want anyone but you. You were a hit."

"Point taken. But when we get home, you are stripping, and I'm spanking your butt, then making sweet love to you."

"Mmm." She accepted his kiss eagerly. "Can we start now?"

"Nope, because we are babysitting. But when I get you home, you know what to do."

"Yes."

"I love you baby and you don't have to belabor this point. I'm a believer. I said I'd buy you a ring."

"I love you too, but I want a proposal to go with a ring."

"Duly noted."

Chapter 10

B ecky stretched luxuriously as she woke to an empty bed. She often did because Carter was up with the chickens, doing drills or PT with his team, or going solo in his home gym. None of the men, or women for that matter, used a public gym because of the exposure. In fact, most of their adult lives had been in the shadows or doing things that absolutely didn't draw attention to themselves or what was theirs. It was a life-long habit.

These men of theirs were not exhibitionists. The attention they drew from the women who wanted them to hang on their trophy walls and the men who wanted to prove their prowess by challenging them was not worth it. Becky now appreciated that Carter was so careful.

Becky was a typically private person, and that didn't bother her. At the beginning of their relationship, Carter tried to keep things quiet. "I don't want others to poke fun or make jokes about you or our relationship. We rib each other all the time, but sometimes, the younger guys don't seem to understand that it can be in poor taste."

She was surrounded by nosy, opinionated guys who thought it was acceptable to point out the errors in her food choices, her exercise habits or lack thereof, her friends, her driving style, and anything they perceived as not the best choices for her. Carter had stepped in and stopped all that, but he took over in a big way. When he let it be known that they were an item, dating, whatever they were calling things at the time, he was all in, and it felt like a claiming, and he was his own protection squad.

Her bottom was still a little achy from his discussion about her demonstration with Storm, but that was okay. He got the message. They were going to set the date sometime soon. Carter, Levi, and Callie were on a protection job that Becky feared Garrett or Jac would put their foot down over. It was a simple bodyguard job, for a VIP couple.

The raised voices behind the conference room door yesterday about a female on a protection detail did nothing to intimidate Becky or the meeting attendees. Carter was concerned when Callie was chosen to go with them, but when it was obviously a good call, and Callie was all in, he backed her. Becky loved Carter's ability to see the whole picture in most situations. He was easygoing when she needed him to be unbiased, so long as it didn't involve her health or safety.

It was a two-man job but having Callie there was a plus. Carter would fly his plane again. They never could find who tampered with the wiring, or who got in past their security to do it. Everything was boosted and they dropped the pass cards and used biotechnology to enter. Carter still left early to check everything.

With four days dedicated to this job, Becky planned on enjoying the freedom being alone would give her. She loved Carter, but some days, not having the expectations of being on task or minding his words and rules was necessary for their relationship. No expectations. That's what she needed right now. She ate cookies, had flavored noodles for dinner, colored, watched a comedy, and had coffee after dinner. Carter called just as she was about to get her PJs on.

"Hey, baby. Are you behaving?"

Becky smiled, and it flavored her tone of voice. "Of course, I'm being good. Are you?"

"Brat. You sound like you are having too much fun. Are you at home?"

"Yep, and I was about to get my PJs on."

"I'm not in the right spot, or I'd play with you some before you changed. I'm outside a fancy hotel grabbing everyone's dinner. Phone sex might get me arrested out here."

"Aren't I worth the risk?"

"Damn straight, but Levi and Callie might get pissed if they don't get dinner."

"Fine. I'll take one for the team. Hey, so are you back Sunday?"

"Monday. We have some follow-up things and will need to retrieve our extra tech equipment from the hotel, and they won't be available to do that until Monday. But it's just a few hours' difference. The job ends Sunday evening. Late."

"Okay. I thought I'd run to see my dad and figure this mess out with the inventory, then give the rest of the information to the accountant and come home. That will take it off my list."

"Can't you do that over the phone? I'm not happy about you going alone. Can one of the girls go with you?"

"I'll check, but really, I'll be fine. I'll go Friday night, spend Saturday and come home Sunday afternoon. Then be ready for work Monday morning."

"Well, let me know before you go. Text me. And turn on your auto-cam so I can check on you when I am able."

"You mean check in on me."

"Same thing. Look, gotta go. Love you with my whole heart and soul. Talk soon. Good night."

"Love you too. Night."

Becky was insightful and very capable, but she'd acknowledged long ago that in her relationship, she would much rather be cared for, than be the caretaker. But when your father needs help figuring things out in his business, what's a daughter to do but help?

Carter wouldn't like that she didn't ask any of the women to go to Tennessee with her, but they had their own lives. The other men were home this weekend. She was doing her friends a favor by not making it a hard decision when she knew they would want to stay home with their men but also feel someone should go with her.

Besides, Ivy had weekend classes to teach. Sharlee had Storm. Jessie was big and pregnant, and Mallory was pukey pregnant. Callie was with Carter and Levi. So, really, no one could go. She didn't know any of the other women at the bookkeeping office, of which there were four, well enough to ask them. Yes, that made great logical sense. Even if Carter would likely not want to agree, how could he not?

Leaving work at three so she would be at her parent's house before dark was a nod to her man. He would approve of this decision. He would also be happy when he found she had her camera on. She had her text-to-voice set up on Bluetooth. Her car had all these fancy tech bells and whistles. At times like this, she was glad Carter insisted on getting her a high-end vehicle.

Carter texted her the minute she pulled into her parent's large circular drive. "Glad you made it there safely. I don't see any passenger with you."

"Well, hello my love. Followed me all the way to Mom and Dad's, did you? You were my passenger. How was your day?"

His message was, "Hmm..." She translated that to be a grunt.

"Okay, I'm going into the house now. Love you. Talk later."

Becky turned off the car and climbed out before he could respond. He did anyway. Her text notification on her phone pinged. She glanced down.

"Need a spanking already?"

She wouldn't answer that. Not now, anyway. She wanted to send a tongue poking out at him, but her man's usual response was to put that tongue to good use, after he spanked her for sticking it out. That was a hard pass right now. Raised libido was not a good idea with him so far away.

The heavy front door opened, and Becky was engulfed in her mother's arms. Candace Carrington wasn't one to meddle in her husband's affairs, work or otherwise, so Becky didn't bother asking her about business things. She also wasn't a hugger, so it was a bit of an odd start to the visit.

Instead of dwelling on those things, Becky let her mother lead her into the spacious kitchen to sit and listen to all the family and neighborhood gossip. Becky had been raised in this house since the age of six. That meant she knew every person her mother was sharing about. It made for an entertaining couple of hours as her mother cooked a late dinner.

Her father, James Carrington, had made dinner come later and later, with his long work hours, Candace shrugged it off and had adjusted. While her mother plied her with bits of dinner while she cooked to stave off hunger, like she did when Becky was little, they talked. Candace never rushed her father or ate before he arrived to sit down with her.

"How is Dad these days?"

Candace hesitated before responding for the first time since Becky walked in the door. "I'm sure he's fine, but I worry he is too stressed. I want him to retire but he says he isn't ready to sell the business."

"Maybe Uncle Karl would buy it from him."

"No, your father has already suggested that, but Karl guilted him into staying another year. But that year is almost up, and I guess I want him to enjoy his retirement years."

"Do you want me to help with some suggestions for retiring?"

"Would you? I know he listens to you. Maybe you could give him some ideas of what he could do with his years outside of work. Maybe play with his grandchildren?"

"I saw what you did there, Mom."

Candace smiled. "I had to try."

"Mama, Carter and I will get married and have children when we are ready and not before. I have a sister you could try to convince."

"You know Trish would die before messing up her figure. You don't need to worry about that." Candace looked up to see Becky's face. "Because your boyfriend doesn't care."

"Nice try, mom. Carter says I'm beautiful." When Candace didn't respond, Becky sighed. "Besides, Carter is pretty busy with his job, and I work full-time too. We'd have to modify things a little. No, a lot."

"Sacrifices for our family are always worth it."

"When you're ready."

"You're over thirty years old. How long before you think that will happen? Your baby clock is ticking."

"Mom, I'm thirty-two. I have a friend who is almost forty and is having a baby. She doesn't think she's too old."

"Well, all I'm saying is there isn't a need to still raise children at sixty."

"Mama, you do know that Carter is almost forty, right? Even if we have a child in the next year, Carter will be 59 when he or she is twenty. And if we have more..." She let her shrug finish the sentence.

"Well, and if he isn't healthy, there is no telling if he'll even be alive then."

"Mama. Stop. And would you think about what you're saying? Do you remember what Carter looks like? Does for a living?"

"I know he's one of those security guys, but I've seen some pretty unhealthy-looking ones. Besides, it doesn't take long to lose that physique. I'm just saying youth does help when raising children. You might think about that yourself. Since you've been with Carter, I know you've been eating better, but are you getting any exercise?"

Becky's mom was five foot nothing and weighed about one hundred pounds soaking wet. But she didn't have her mother's body type like her sister Trish, who was a naturally slender but taller version of their mother. Becky was fluffy, cuddly, and soft, just as Carter liked her.

Candace never was a nurturer. She made sure all your needs were met but as far as the parent you snuggled up with, that wasn't her. Becky realized while her father was the more fun parent growing up, she didn't have hugging parents. Not like she and Carter would be with any kids they had.

"You know how you are when you get comfortable in your life."

"Right, and we are done with this conversation."

"Well, think about it. I'm only saying it to help you in the future."

Time for a subject change. "Mom, do you think Dad is still at the office?"

"Probably. Why don't you call him and find out when we'll have dinner? It's time he came home at a normal hour with his daughter here to visit."

"I think I will. Be right back."

As she punched in the phone number, she saw a new SUV pull into the drive. She knew it wasn't her dad because he never bought any big ticket item new. He bought it slightly used. "Better value."

Knowing that about her dad, Becky expected that it was her Uncle Karl in the showy vehicle, and that was confirmed when a man that exuded money and arrogance stepped out of the car. Becky put on a cautious smile and hung up when the call to her father went to voice mail.

Karl plastered on a smile that never seemed to reach his eyes and reached out his arms to encourage a hug. Becky, never one to make others feel awkward, put on a brittle smile and went in for a hug. She controlled the shudder of distaste at his cologne and pushed through the residual feeling of being dirty as she stepped back. He was never a favorite relative.

"I've been invited for dinner, and I believe James is behind me. He'll be here in a few minutes. Let's get in out of the cold and catch up."

Becky headed in with her uncle, frantically deciding if she should tell him what she was worried about or just show up tomorrow at the warehouse and do the inventory. She decided to do what she had learned from the people she worked with; keep your information close to your chest and only reveal it if necessary.

"Sure, I'd love to know how your family is doing."

Thanks to her mom, she knew her aunt had just left him, and the divorce was already a bitter fight. No loss to the family, but his kids were struggling with it. She knew there had been trouble for years, but since their kids were about ten years younger than Becky, it wasn't as easy for young adults when their parents separated. Karl and his wife waited until the last child was no longer home and then called it quits. Her mom had said it was time and it looked like she was right. Karl was as pompous as ever.

Just as they crossed the threshold, James Carrington drove into the driveway and parked his modest but well-cared-for Buick Encore behind Becky. It was a perfect size for him and his mom, except without the hefty price tag. Her mother had a small Ford Focus just for her own running around. They weren't flashy people like her uncle.

"Princess!"

"Dad!"

She had never called him Daddy and now, when she had her own loving Daddy, it made it less awkward. She didn't design it this way, but James Carrington had never liked to be called anything but Dad as an endearment, so she had always used Dad. It now worked out perfectly.

"What are you doing here? Did I know you were coming?"

"I told you this morning, but you must have been very busy." Becky worried about his memory more and more. Maybe it was too much stress. She knew that might keep you in a fog sometimes.

"Yes, I must have been to have forgotten my best girl was coming."

Dinner was full of conversation and the night ended by ten. The following morning, bright and early before anyone was up at the house, and certainly before anyone was at the warehouse, Becky went to take inventory with her father's self-tabulating, handheld counting machine. She set it up to go to the cloud account she'd created for her father's books. She placed everything in there. If she ran into trouble, she could recreate the whole scenario.

First, she took a video of the whole warehouse and its inventory. The shelves were neatly stacked, and where there seemed to be any chaos or jumbled stock, she took a closer video to review later. By seven a.m., she was ready to begin the count. She was nearly half done when she took a coffee break. She'd done her uncle's side first in case he protested that she shouldn't do his. She would compare everything later. Right now, she needed to finish the second half.

This new technology in doing the inventory was excellent. Becky's father was the kind of guy who did it the old-fashioned way for most things, but she applauded his giving into this improvement. It helped her immeasurably. When her father and uncle showed up by nine, she was done except for the closets.

When the door opened, she had almost finished the last large storage closet, and her uncle walked in.

She quickly uploaded everything in the scanner, sent a message to Sharlee for safekeeping, and waited.

"Becky, we know you are in here, and while you think you have found something off, you are wrong. I didn't want to tell you how bad your father's memory has gotten lately, but he has relied on the warehouse manager and me to take care of things."

Becky debated whether she should come out or not, but she decided against it. Her father forgot a few messages and lost track of time more than in his younger days, but when they spoke about things pertaining to business and investments, he tracked just fine. Becky resolved to check his investment portfolios too. All his finances would need a good going over. She'd get Jessie to help her understand some of that later.

The door closed behind Karl as he continued to other parts of the building, presumably to find her. Thank goodness the building's overhead lights came on with the main switch, so he could only guess if she were in a closet. They called them closets, and they were numbered, but really, they were storage rooms with a specific inventory. It was easier to find things when the store had grown.

Finally, all done, everything uploaded, everything sent to one of Sharlee's many mailboxes as a backup; Becky stepped out of the room. She didn't see anyone, so she went into the warehouse office and poured herself another cup of coffee, relieved she'd finished in record time and that everyone was late on Saturday mornings.

Her father wandered into the office within ten minutes, followed by the manager. She didn't ask where her uncle was but knew he wasn't far behind. "Got what you needed?" asked Monty, his warehouse manager. "I think so. Is there any inventory in other places besides the main warehouse and four closets?"

"Nope, except for the things your uncle keeps in his closet, but I think most of that is his private property."

James turned to Monty. "His private property, like household items? Garage overflow? What?"

"I honestly don't know. He had it padlocked with a key." said Monty.

James grunted.

Becky stood in the stockroom, staring at the shelves of products she had counted. On her father's side, the numbers today matched the numbers from last quarter, except for one corner, next to Karl's section. After considering that things were bought and sold, it was the number she had expected, and the overflow was from that segment that didn't seem to hold inventory from her father. Maybe they were mixed up. But these were not the numbers on the books. Why? Something was wrong. She cleared the information and removed where they had been uploaded to. She reset everything.

The inventory numbers had been tampered with, and she could feel the knot in her stomach growing tighter with each passing moment. Why would anyone want her father's inventory numbers to look inflated? Why not just put Karl's inventory on his own count?

She turned to her father, who seemed confused about why the numbers didn't add up. Her uncle simply blew her off. "It's been a while since you've taken inventory, and you've likely forgotten how to do it. Besides, that new counter isn't as accurate as hand counting."

But Becky knew that wasn't the case. She knew how to take inventory, and the counter was more accurate. It didn't lose count, and she scanned each box. "Well, no worries. We'll figure things out. My friend is a forensic accountant, so I'll take things to her, and she'll be able to see where the mistake is quickly. I'm going to the house to get breakfast. You want to come with me, Dad?"

"Sure, I could eat."

"Great. Nice to meet you, Monty. See you next trip, Uncle. Next time I'll bring Carter."

"Your big brawny guy." her uncle asked sarcastically.

"Yep, my big, brawny, Special Operations pilot, bodyguard guy." Monty and James laughed, but Uncle Karl didn't even crack a smile.

"You do that," he said before he walked away.

Chapter 11

H er worst fears were confirmed as Becky rechecked the inventory after returning to her parent's house. The numbers were significantly off, and the merchandise seemed wrong. She could feel it in her bones. If the men had asked about where the numbers were off or any kind of clarification, she might think it was a colossal mistake, but the warehouse manager nor her uncle said a word and her father just shook his head in confusion. Something fishy was at play, and she was determined to get to the bottom of it.

Carter had texted her several times but with the phone on mute, so she wasn't disturbed, she hadn't known. She cringed as the texts started light and sweet, and by the time the last text came in at ten a.m. when she turned the ring and notifications back on, his messages had a dark tinge.

Carter: Rebecca Shea, if you don't answer me by lunchtime, I will send Monroe and his rubber paddle your way with permission to use it.

Becky: Sorry, sorry. I was doing inventory and didn't want anyone to disturb me. You know how the girls are when you are out of town, calling me non-stop, trying to convince me to stay with them, and now that we are both gone this weekend, I avoided their loving annoyance. I certainly wouldn't have gotten things done early.

Carter: Are you done now?

Becky: Yes.

Carter: Sir.

Becky: Daddy

Carter: I want a check-in every three hours during the day, and do not leave without telling me and turning on the camera.

Becky: I won't. I promise.

Carter: Be good. I love you.

Becky: I'm always good. I love you too. Bye.

The rest of the afternoon was spent shopping with her mother, visiting some of the neighbors who came to say hello, and texting Carter at the appropriate intervals.

"He is kind of needy, isn't he?"

"Who," asked Becky after sending her third check-in text.

"Your Carter. You are always texting him."

"It probably seems like that, but really, that isn't the case. I just sent him information about what we are doing. He likes to know about my day. And he isn't within close distance. He's on a job, and I'm here. Two different directions. I told you about the incident with the snowplow. He's just protective."

"We don't see you as often as we used to."

"Mom, that isn't true. Before Carter and I got together, I came about three times a year unless there was a purpose. I've already been here three times in three months. I came at Christmas and stayed the whole week, and the first of February and I'm here now, and it's just the beginning of March. Last year I didn't show up until June, so it's not Carter that determines whether I come or stay home. It has everything to do with my work schedule and what I'm doing in my life."

"Well, it just seems like he has a leash on you, and I don't like it." Candice reached over and patted her daughter on the knee. "But that's okay; one of these days, you'll have children and won't need to work. Then you'll be able to come and visit more often."

Becky decided not to burst her bubble, but if she had children, she'd be busier than she was now. And she would need Carter for a conversation of that magnitude. Visits would likely be relegated to big holidays and swapping out with Carter's family. But there was no reason to cross a bridge that hadn't been built yet.

Sharlee called around ten the following day. "Are you sitting down?"

"Well, good morning, Sharlee, and no, I was standing and packing my bag. Do I need to sit down?"

"I guess it doesn't make any difference whether you're sitting or standing but don't get in your car."

"Come again?"

"Don't get in your car. Don't let anyone get in any car. Sharp Security is on their way to check out the vehicles at your parents' place. Someone was on the property, and while we couldn't see everything, it appears that they were fiddling with stuff, the cars or something."

"How did you see that?" asked Becky. Her suspicion was heard loudly in her question and tone.

"You might well ask. Carter and Jac were behind this one. And in this case, as it is all too often, they were right on the money."

"What made them want to check things out?"

"Gut instinct, I'm told, and you never discount your gut. When you aren't the only one with that feeling, it's a certainty. So, they had me tap into your parents' security. Don't they ever check their feed?"

"Guess not enough. Isn't that against the law or something?"

"If there is a complaint, we could get our hands slapped, but since you aren't going to tell anyone, no one will know. Besides, I know you remember the fiasco when they had my apartment and parking lot rigged for video and sound. Congratulations, you have joined the women with hot but over-protective lovers club."

"But how will I explain that Nick's crew is out here doing the car scans?"

"Tell your parents you thought you heard something last night and get them to check the feed. Then pretend you're calling help in. You work for the most well-known security company for most people who care."

"Good point. Okay. I'll do it but I gotta go and do it fast."

Becky jumped up from the edge of the bed and headed for her dad's office. She remembered how to work the security camera, and sat watching the recording when her dad came in.

"Becky, what's wrong? Why are you looking at the camera feed?"

"Oh, hi Dad. I thought I heard something last night but was too tired to do more than acknowledge I heard a sound. So, this morning, I thought I'd follow up. Look what I found."

James sat down beside his daughter to watch. "You know, I forget we have this most of the time."

After a couple more minutes, they saw a person with a hoodie and a ski mask, sweats, and sweatshirt drop down between the cars, then, in no time, they were running out of the camera shot.

"I need to call the police."

"No, I already called a company we have worked with on several occasions. Sharp Security. They are much closer than our company. They should be here pretty quick."

The doorbell rang right at that moment. "Becky, there are some security people here to speak to you. What's going on?"

Becky stopped to throw on her sweats and a long-sleeved tee while her father went down to let them do their thing. She shoved her feet into her sneakers without socks and asked her mom to make coffee.

"I already did, dear. I know how to entertain even if the guests are people I've never met before." Becky ignored the message her mother was trying to send and headed for the front door.

Nick Sharp was a nice-looking man with the confidence only found in dangerous jobs and orchestrating those jobs. He was similar to Jac in certain ways and then not at all like him. She would have been intimidated by his presence if she hadn't been working on projects that had brought them on board with some of their teams in the last year. As it was, she just saw him as another hot security guy. He was not as sizzling as her guy, but he had assets.

She reached her hand out. "Nick. I didn't know they were pulling out the big guns."

"Rebecca." He had Jac as a name reference, so she didn't correct him. "Surprised to see you here and with this issue. Where's Carter?"

"On a job. This is my parents' house. I guess you met my father, James Carrington."

"I did. He told me you heard something last night and pulled up the feed. Smart."

They both knew that Sharlee had caught the intruder and that she had called them, but if they were going to keep the fact that the information was gotten by not entirely legal means, it had to be this way.

Just then, Becky received a text. Nick grinned. "Carter or Jac?"

"Carter. Excuse me while I get read the riot act and then reassure him. That is if I can reassure him."

"We've taken care of the issue, and your dad and I are discussing the type of security he needs in this upscale neighborhood."

"Okay, I'll let Carter know, and you guys keep talking but inside. Mom has coffee cake and coffee if you want it."

"Come on in, Nick and Jared. Let's talk security while my daughter does her thing."

Becky followed and walked to her room to chat with Carter. Her hands shook, realizing someone had tried tampering with her car. She didn't know exactly what was done, only that they had.

Carter: Baby, are you all right?

Becky: I'm okay. Who would tamper with my car?

Carter: Working on that answer right now. I am finishing this job tonight, but I'll be home in the morning. Garrett is on his way to pick you up. Nick and Jared will take your car back with them and find out as much as they can from it before bringing it up to us. Your parents' cars weren't tampered with.

Becky: I can just wait until they finish to go home. I'm sure Jac will understand.

Carter: Jac won't understand, and I will paddle your bare bottom raw if you don't come home now. You can stay with Ivy or Sharlee. We'll get the car back in a couple of days. I have to go, but you do not leave alone. Wait for Garrett to pick you up, or I will be very angry.

Becky: Fine.

Carter: I know you're upset but watch the tone.

Becky: I'm going now. There is no tone with one-word texts. See you tomorrow.

Things went fast after that. Candace tried to make the men breakfast, but they declined. And within thirty minutes of Nick Sharp and Jared showing up, Garrett was parking his car on the street. He looked around as though taking in the lay of the land, just like Carter had done when he first came to her parents' house. These men.

When he strode like he was king of the world up to the front door, another trait all these alpha men seemed to have, Becky's mother hesitated as she stared at the big, secret service-looking man.

"Mrs. Carrington? I'm Garrett Sullivan, and I've come to retrieve Rebecca."

"Garrett?" The minute she heard a familiar voice, Becky knew she had revealed her feelings of being out of her depth and needed someone she trusted to take things over.

"Becky, you know this man?"

Her smile was one of amused relief. "Oh, yeah, I know him."

Candace backed away from the door to allow the new man entrance. Garrett hugged Becky tight, letting her go when he was sure she wasn't too upset with the morning's events. He kissed the top of her head, placing his arm around her shoulders.

"Honey, I'm not sure Carter would be happy that you are hugging another man," said Candace as she watched the scene unfold in her living room. "Or that he was kissing you."

"What? Don't be ridiculous. Mom and Dad, I'd like you to meet Garrett Sullivan. He is one of the owners of the company I work for and..."

"And Carter is my brother in every way that counts. He sent me to pick Becky up and take her home."

"But can't she just drive her own car home?" Her mother didn't seem to understand the severity of the almost incident. "And isn't she important enough for him to come and get her?"

Becky opened her mouth to inform her mother, but Garrett put his hand on her arm, stopping her words. His stern expression told her that he was going to handle it. She was well-versed in how these men took the lead.

"Because of the tampering of her car, we can't have her driving it until we have the full forensics off the undercarriage and go over it with a fine-toothed comb. Nick and Jared's company will do that for us. And Carter is on an important job and won't be done before very late tonight so he won't be home until tomorrow."

"Oh," said Becky's mother. "But what will she drive to work?"

Garrett calmly explained no one would ever leave her stranded, ever. His calm, authoritative voice and manner seemed to have spellbound her mother, and Becky needed to break that ill-fated attraction or whatever it was. Callie's man could look highly sophisticated, and Becky was glad he impressed her mom. It would stop her from asking too many questions.

Nick and Jared spoke to Garrett after Candace Carrington was satisfied with the answers he gave her. They had finished talking to James about security moments before Garrett had arrived. As the men were thanking Candace for the coffee and hospitality, Becky reached for her keys left on the side table. Before she realized it, Garrett had his hand on hers, and his voice spoke low and sternly close to her ear.

"If you don't want your backside warmed the minute you leave today, I suggest you return the keys to the table and let Sharp take the car to assess it."

Becky whispered back bitingly. "I'm Carter's, and you don't get to punish me."

His smile was almost evil. "You keep thinking that little girl. When it comes to health and safety, the standard rules don't apply. You know that. Now put them back, little one."

Becky replaced the keys. The thing was, he spoke the truth. These overprotective men had gotten in her way so often that it had become everyday life for her to be more careful and listen to their directions. Not always, but since they'd found women of their own, they had become more intense and protective. It was reminiscent of musk ox males surrounding the females. It was infuriating that it made her feel special and seen. Sharlee said it was because they had more to lose if they weren't dili-gent. Becky thought it was just part of their makeup.

"Good girl. Now, are you ready to go home?"

"Almost. Honestly, why can't I drive my own car? They re-moved the device."

"That they could see. There are other things that could help them find out who did this. Signature designs, or other things. You know that. Go ahead and finish getting ready, and I'll walk the guys out and get the official rundown on your car before they take off with it."

It had been a quick goodbye, but Becky was ready for the weekend to end anyway. This visit had been full of surprises, from the inventory and how people acted to her being there, the words Uncle Karl had said about her father, and the man-ager's not-quite-truthful aura. Then the tampering with her car turned out to be an incendiary device, with more yet to be learned, that put paid to her enjoyment. She was glad she didn't have to drive home but wouldn't share that bit.

"Kaden's or Jac's?"

"Pardon?"

Garrett asked, "You doing okay?"

"Sure."

"Don't be worried about what happened. We'll figure it out."

"I know, but I can't help wondering if they targeted me or if this was another random, could have killed me, thing."

Garrett audibly inhaled and released a deep sigh. "You know what we think about coincidences. However, it was in two different places, weeks apart."

"What are the odds?"

"Not good for random, but it doesn't mean they weren't. Just means we dig deeper."

"Did you talk to Carter today?" asked Becky.

"Yep. I wouldn't plan on any alone time in the near future," he said cheerfully.

"Great," Becky groaned.

But she was strangely okay with that scenario because the alternative would leave her alone and vulnerable, two things she was never very fond of. And after this weekend, she was even less enthused to be alone.

"Jac's. Ivy and Kaden are gone, remember."

"Yes, but they will be home tonight if you'd like Sharlee or Jac to run you to their house."

"I'm good."

"Okay, we'll go to Jac's then."

"Just drop me off so you don't have to use up any more of your day. Thanks for coming to get me, Garrett."

"Sweetheart, I'm your watchdog until your Daddy comes home. Didn't he tell you?"

"No."

"Sorry, but that's the way it's going to be. I don't mind watching Jac's big-ass television, but I'm sure you would have instead done something else.

Great, just great. Now she had Jac, Sharlee, and Garrett keeping watch. She guessed she could even count Finley if she needed to even the numbers. Life had just gotten more complicated than she had ever wanted it. The tears were never far from the surface, but she had been able to keep them at bay... so far.

Her cell rang. "Carter?"

"Hey, Baby Bear. I only have a minute, but I had to break away to hear your voice. Are you with Garrett and are you okay?"

"Yes. And I don't get to go home."

"I know sweetheart. I'll be home as soon as I can."

"Okay."

"Sorry baby, I have to go. Love you."

"Love you too."

Mini Fort Knox is what Jacquard Reynaud lived in, but he refused to admit it was overboard. The security guards at the entrance of the property had been waiting for them because when Garrett drove into the entrance drive, the gate opened automatically, and they waved as the car passed them. Sharlee met the two of them at the door.

Her boss's words echoed in her head as got out of Garrett's car. "My family will always feel safe here. The one with my name and the one I have created through blood, sweat, and tears. I'm unwilling to lose any of them through lack of safety measures."

That same Jac met them at the door behind his wife, Sharlee. Becky loved working for Jac and being part of the team-based family he'd created. The sense of belonging was none she had ever experienced or seen anywhere else, but after talking to Nick Sharp a little, she thought it might be that way with his people.

"Rebecca, let me know what is happening as you see it. What did you do at your parents' house? Jessie told Mark it had to do with accounting and inventory?"

"Okay, can't a girl get a cup of coffee before she has to bare her soul?"

"Saucy today, aren't you?"

Garrett followed with her computer bag and her overnight case. "All morning."

"Yeah, well, you would be too if, instead of having an easy visit with your folks, you ended up with a weird uncle, crazy inventory, bombs, and G-men everywhere."

"G-men?" Jac and Garrett laughed.

"Hey, this G-man bought you breakfast."

"Thank you for breakfast, mean ol' G-man. He threatened to spank me."

"Extraordinary circumstances call for out-of-the-box solutions. Normal rules don't apply," Jac spoke as though it was a pre-recorded message.

"That's what I told her," said Garrett.

Becky rolled her eyes.

"Come on, let's get you some coffee," said Sharlee as she looped her arm into Becky's and headed for the coffee nook in the corner of the kitchen, giggling as they went.

Later that night, Becky was tired, but she couldn't sleep. She'd been jittery and jumpy, and she missed Carter so much she was on the edge of crying. Jac had been on the phone a few hours ago, and while Becky thought he was talking to Carter, he didn't offer to share his phone, so it probably wasn't him. One more night was all she had to get through. Carter would be here first thing in the morning.

She knew he would be here as soon as he could. It just wasn't soon enough. Becky hadn't felt so out of control of her life since she left home and embarked on adulthood. Once she was hired to be Jac's assistant seven years ago, she hadn't felt unprotected.

Since she and Carter had gotten together, she only felt empowered, and her natural sassiness had returned. She was safe in her world, secure in the knowledge that Carter and the others would always protect her. Until a few weeks ago nothing had been able to shake that reality.

This morning all that changed. Today had demonstrated to Becky that she was vulnerable, and Carter wouldn't always be there. She'd resisted learning to do more than fire the pistol, but now she decided being proficient was important. She had always been afraid of touching the gun Jac had painstakingly found that fit her hand the best. She rarely carried it with her except for the times that she knew Jac would be asking, and even then, she kept it closed up and safe. But now, things would be very different. She would bring it with her, and Carter would help her figure out the best way to do that.

Carter expected her to know how to protect herself and agreed with Jac that everyone needed to know how to defend themselves in a dire emergency. The hardest thing would be getting used to that woman. She'd always been easygoing. Do what the majority wanted to do if you could. A don't rock the boat kind of girl, she had always expected her boyfriend to be the kind of man to stand in the gap so she didn't have to, but this weekend that wouldn't work.

She'd sign up for one of Ivy's classes to get hands-on experience with self-defense classes. Sometimes she wouldn't have a gun or Carter or any of the other guys. If she was attacked on the street, she'd need to know how to survive. The guys would be happy, but would she?

Becky shook it off. It wasn't about having a carefree, responsible life anymore. It was about survival. She couldn't be the sweet little submissive for Carter anymore. She needed to toughen up and get a handle on things. She'd always been self-sufficient, but that didn't seem like enough. Would Carter even want her if she wasn't his baby girl anymore? Because she wasn't sure that that was someone she was, after being attacked with a load of snow and then someone trying to blow her up. Maybe being sweet and easygoing was the problem.

Becky didn't know if she could be anyone else but would give it a damn good try. Even her mind stuttered when she swore mentally because Carter would not be okay with that. The other guys would have lifted an eyebrow, at least, because that wasn't the person she'd always been. But maybe she should be more like Sharlee and Callie. Tougher on the outside so she didn't expose her soft underbelly. And maybe she needed to work on that underbelly, too.

Becky was so confused she didn't know what she would do or how she should act, but something had to change. Carter would say it wasn't she who had to change, but how they reacted to the world, their preparation would need to be more diligent. It was too much for her to figure out; she just needed her Daddy. Maybe that part of her had to go away too, and the thought devastated her.

It was the only place she could switch off her mind because even when they had friend time or enjoyed each other's company in the group, her mind continually ran in the background. Maybe that's how everyone's worked, but she didn't think so. Ivy didn't seem concerned about life, except Ivy was rich and younger than her. Those things might have had something to do with it, or perhaps it was just her personality. She wasn't sure that Callie turned off either, and she hadn't seen much of Jessie lately since she was at the end of her pregnancy, and Mark kept her pretty protected at all times.

She sighed. Maybe a swim would clear the utter chaos in her mind because now that she had given in to the swirling thoughts and fears, she was hopelessly awake.

Chapter 12

Becky was in the dressing room finishing up after her swim, she was now physically exhausted as well as mentally and emotionally depleted. She was thinking that she needed to have Carter back when heavy footsteps echoed in the pool room. Turning to the door, she grabbed her towel and threw it in the hamper before heading for the exit. Standing in the doorway was her man. Big, intimidating, worried.

"Baby, are you alright?"

Becky knew that concerned, loving voice, and she dropped the swimsuit in her hand and leaped into his arms. She would have taken him to the ground if he hadn't been such a large man. His massive muscles and height would necessitate more than her jumping in his arms to take him off balance.

"You're here? How? It's not tomorrow."

"The job ended, and I left the clean-up to Callie and Levi. I did my job until the end, but it was the hardest thing I've done in a while. I didn't want to. After we escorted our clients to their flight, and watched the plane take off, I immediately shifted from work to Daddy mode." Carter sighed as he held her tight.

"Carter, breathing here." He loosened his hold and kissed her temple.

"Daddy. I was so scared. Expect me to dog you for a very long time. I love you. I nearly dropped everything to get to you when I discovered you had a fucking device on your car. I still can't believe it." His tortured tones changed to fierceness. Daddy Teddy Bear was back. "You will never be out of my sight again," he said sternly.

It wasn't possible, but it was a nice sentiment. Becky smiled. "I missed you, too."

"Baby, I need to know everything."

"Okay, but if I do explain it all, you have to tell everyone else. I'm tired of repeating myself."

He moved his hands from under her butt to her waist, allowing her to slide down his body before pulling her in tight. "You'll tell it as often as you need to so we can catch the asshole who tried to hurt my girl. I'll take care of you, baby. We all will. This isn't going to end well for those fuckers, whoever they are. I need you to know that there won't be any 'you are forgiven' fairytales to be seen here. There won't be any pink princesses and magnanimous gestures from Prince Charming. They are going down as painfully as I can manage."

Becky could feel herself get lost in the depths of Carter's eyes as he took charge. His stormy blue gaze was powerful and protective and spoke to her battered nerves loud and clear, *it will be okay*. Even feeling the fear that now seemed to run continuously in the background, with Carter, she could feel the comfort and confidence radiating from him through his firm, soothing voice, and it did the trick. She was surrounded by his love, and she relaxed.

"You are never leaving my sight."

"I know, Daddy."

"You are officially in my pocket."

"I know, Daddy."

"I was so scared for you, and I knew it was a hell of a long way for me to get to you."

"I know, Daddy."

"I love you so much, baby girl. I can't lose you."

"I know, Daddy."

Becky knew it wasn't just words or a bluff to make her feel better. This man was hers, and she was his. Carter would take care of her, and all the things that had circled in her head earlier were quieted when she stood next to Carter when he was in his dominant mode. Nothing else mattered right now. Nothing.

CARTER WAS PACING THE conference room like a caged panther. Dark, angry, trapped. He needed at least a few hours in the gym to burn off this energy.

"Carter, have a seat. We have to look at this rationally."

"*Rationally*? Someone tried to *kill* her, Monroe. They tried to fucking *kill* my baby. I need to find who did this and end them. I can't have anyone who would harm Becky on the streets, walking, planning, *breathing!*"

Jac leaned back and let Carter get the worst out of his system. Carter knew it was the way he handled things. For a brief moment, Carter appreciated the autonomy to do what he needed without someone trying to corral him or his expressions of frustration and anger.

Garrett asked after a few moments of quiet. "What can we do to help?"

They all knew the group would take on the task of finding and eliminating the threat to their own, but they also knew, from long experience, that Carter had to be predominately satisfied with the outcome, or he would go rogue. Most of them had been there themselves at least once.

He looked around the room at the men he loved like his brothers. They were tough, protective men that took care of their women fiercely. Becky had been theirs to protect collectively before they or she found a mate. She was there at the beginning of it all at Jacquard and Associates. They would do whatever was necessary to take care of business. Time for their brother to relax enough to let them in and get this done.

Carter sighed heavily. "Okay, let's find these fuckers and take them down."

Jac looked intensely at Sharlee, who had come in for this office meeting, and Sharlee narrowed her eyes as she glared at her husband. "I am not offended by that word, Jac, so stop acting like I'm made of cotton candy."

Jac nodded his head. "Only during business hours." Sharlee gave him a frustrated, exaggerated sigh.

Jac's meaning was clear. Sharlee was his woman, and at all other times, the language would be curtailed, but right now, he didn't say anything in this situation. Carter would have apologized, but sometimes, it was the best way to express oneself, and right now, it was better he was here using profanity than out in the world, setting it on fire. Even though he might do that soon, anyway. For now, at least, fuckers was a placeholder.

Monroe did the Monroe thing. "Okay, let's lay everything that we have thus far on the table, figure out what we need, and then make a plan of action."

"Where is Rebecca?" asked Jac.

"In her office, I imagine," said Levi.

Carter stood. "She was supposed to come in with you, Jac." His tone was tinged with accusation.

"Down, Carter," said an unaffected Jac. "Callie, can you bring Rebecca in, and let's go over again what happened. I have some preliminary findings from Sharp Security."

Callie left to grab Becky from her next-door office. There was a small connecting hallway that had four doors coming off it: Jac's office which also had a back door exit, Becky's office, a conference room, and a private bathroom. Becky's door was the only entrance from the main building and her inner door which opened to the mutual hallway were both set to auto-lock upon closure for her safety. During times like these, it helped and hurt. When Becky didn't open the door at Callie's buzz, Callie moved back to the conference room.

"Any other place she might be other than her office?" she asked.

Carter stood quickly, as did Mark, who was in overdrive mode regarding the protection detail. "Look to see if you can find her in the bathroom," said Mark.

Carter was already at the door and ringing the bell. He punched in the code that Becky had given him and stalked into her office. Nothing. He stalked over to Jac's office. The door was ajar but that was usually how Jac left it. In the corner, against the wall that the door was on, was Becky, crouched with tears running down her cheeks.

"Baby Bear, what's wrong?" He yelled into the outer room. "I found her. She's okay. We'll be out in a few."

Mark stepped inside the door just enough to assess the situation and replied, "I'll let the others know. See you in the conference room shortly."

Carter nodded as he went down on his haunches next to Becky. "Sweetheart, what happened?"

"S-someone called. Th-they said to close m-my m-mouth. Th-they said they were coming for m-me." She sniffed as he picked her up off the floor. "Th-then the outer bell rang." Her fear was tangible. She trembled in his arms, nearly bringing him to his knees. They would pay for what they had done to his sweet, trusting woman. But first identify the "they," and then end them.

"I'm taking you into the conference room. You aren't answering any more phone calls, not your cell phone, not the office phone, no phones. And you're never going to be alone again. If someone wants to play these games, they will play them with me, not you. Maybe if they get the idea that you're no longer available to their harassment or intimidation tactics, they'll come out into the open. But don't you worry. If they don't come out into the open, we'll go into the dark and find them."

Becky nodded as she listened to him and sniffled the last of her tears. Carter grabbed the box of tissue off Jac's credenza as he passed it and patted her face dry. He kissed her lips, snuggled her tight to him, and then set her on her feet again. She needed to walk into the conference room, not as a frightened woman but as one who knew she had backup. She couldn't do that if he carried her in, but it was hard for him not to hold her tight. All he wanted to do was capture her in his arms and lock them away. Carter wrapped his brawny arm around her waist in substitution and supported her while she walked into the conference room.

As they made their way around the table to their seats, Carter filled them in on what Becky had told him.

"Becky, do you want water or tea? Coffee?" asked Callie.

"A good strong drink?" asked Sharlee. "Ow! Jac, wouldn't you want a strong drink if you had something traumatic happen to you?"

Jac grunted, and then when Becky sat in her usual empty seat next to him, and Monroe moved down so Carter could sit next to her, he nodded. Jac's hand reached out and covered Becky's.

"Rebecca, I know this is scary as hell, but we need to go over every moment you can remember about this whole thing starting with the day last month that you girls had a fun night at Ivy's through when Garrett picked you up yesterday morning."

"I think we should add the addition of when Becky started to go over her father's business books," said Garrett.

"Agreed," said Mark. "Jessie said there was something fishy going on there."

Carter set two cold bottles of water on the table, opening and placing one bottle in front of Becky. Her hands were shaking, and Carter wished he'd had a sippy cup that he used when she was recovering last month. No spilling, so it didn't matter how she drank it. It only landed in her mouth.

"Be right back." Carter left the room and quickly returned with her water bottle. Without saying a word, he poured the water into the bottle and put the lid back on it. "Now it will stay cold." But he and Becky knew it was for a different reason.

A way for her man to give her comfort and help her settle into her pampered headspace without announcing it.

She took a slow drink. Carter replaced the water bottle on the table and placed his hand on hers. Jac patted the hand he covered and leaned back into his seat at the head of the table.

After a sigh, she said, "I think I'm okay."

"Okay, now take us through the Ramirez angle," said Jac.

"Well, that all started when Ramirez came at closing time, and instead of turning him away, reception sent him through to Jac. I'm still angry about that."

"That isn't quite what happened, but we will get some re-training scheduled. Go on," said Jac.

Becky nodded. She went on to discuss the goons in the front waiting room, then the guys showing up, and that she had parked in the front lot because she was running late at lunch.

"It would have taken too long to park in the underground lot and walk the length of the building to get to my office. So I parked up front."

Carter made a grumbling sound deep in his chest that always sounded like he was growling. "That won't be happening again," he said.

She went on to describe the conversation that she had overheard while sitting in the car. Then the truck with the snow-plow.

"Then nothing."

Monroe asked, "Tell us why you were at your mom's house?"

Becky took another drink, followed by a deep breath. Carter rubbed the back of her neck to help center her. "Carter was gone on assignment. It made perfect sense to talk to my parents, in person, about the discrepancy in the inventory numbers. I was working the inventory because my dad needed the extra help and didn't think hiring another person was the right answer. He has been having some memory loss or extra fogginess in the last months. Still, he thought something felt "off," but he couldn't pinpoint why he felt that way."

She explained the setup in the pet supply store he ran, and that Becky's Uncle Karl ran a pet store that mostly just sold pets. "Dad has nothing to do with his brother's side of the business and vice versa, except they share a warehouse. Dad uses most of it, and Uncle Karl leases part of it. They have one warehouse manager and one warehouse employee on which they split the salaries."

"So, you went there to figure out the problem?" asked Mark.

"Right. Well, I went mostly because of timing. April is coming up, and Dad's accountant needs the inventory numbers. I did the count from last year's ending numbers, which should have been this year's beginning, and ran it continuously to the end of this fiscal year when a re-inventory was to be done. I knew how much was supposed to be in the warehouse, but there was a huge difference when I compared my numbers to the paperwork totals."

"Could something like a shipment go unrecorded?" asked Garrett.

"Possibly, but the numbers on the paperwork wouldn't even fit in his warehouse. Anyway, after talking to Jessie, I decided that I should do a new inventory. So I went, took pictures and video, and did a digital count of the entire warehouse. Both owners have claimed the inventory was mixed."

"Wow, that's a lot of work," said Garrett.

"Not as much because there isn't a huge variety of items and I know that place and where things are by memory."

"And was it mixed?" asked Levi.

"Not that I could tell, but I haven't been able to sit with Jessie and ensure I did everything right. I mean, I used to do the inventory, so I know what I'm doing, but it's good to have another set of eyes, and she is a forensic accountant, so that makes it even better. Another thing is my uncle already knew I was questioning the numbers, and he tried to make it sound like I didn't know what I was doing. When I said I was working with a forensic accountant to make sure things were accurate, he was not happy."

Mark nodded. "Jessie is excited to do something since she is bored on bed rest."

Callie looked confused. "So, is this linked to the first incident, or are they two separate things?"

Kaden shook his head. "Sharlee and I have been reviewing the videotape, and honestly, I don't think it is a coincidence."

"Right," said Sharlee. "They are linked somehow, but are they linked because she stumbled into something fishy at her dad's warehouse or because she overheard something that Ramirez said he doesn't want to be repeated?"

"Or both," said Callie.

"Or neither," said Garrett.

"Agreed. You all know what to do. Track that phone call from this morning. Then find out who Ramirez might have been calling that day he was in the parking lot. Kaden and Sharlee are on the video, with details of both incidents. Bring me some scenarios or suspects or something."

"Jac, I won't answer the phones. Just let me stay in the office and work. Carter can bring me. I won't drive in."

Jac looked over at Carter and did the guy communication thing that Becky could not interpret, even after all these years. Carter squeezed her knee and then rubbed her thigh. Jac didn't respond to her interruption.

"Mark, I need you and Carter to back each other up for Jessica and Rebecca. Backgrounds on everyone that might be involved with any of this and their close associates while keeping the women safe. If you need my house, use it. There are few—"

"Jac, wait," said Becky. "I can't put Jessie in any danger. She's pregnant, for God's sake. I'll just do this alone."

"No, you won't, and if you interrupt me again, there will be consequences. Am I clear?"

"Cranky much? I'm just doing my job."

Jac rubbed his face and then leaned close to hers. "Rebecca, we have a long history, and I love you like a sister, so if you think I won't follow through just because Carter is here, you are operating under a false rainbow."

Becky had been Jac's only female employee on the team or frontlines for a few years before Sharlee or Jessie's jobs existed in house, and she knew what consequences meant with this bunch. They had pretty much left her alone on that score but that had been because she was usually quietly working behind the lines. Jac waited for a moment, and then he went on.

"Garrett and Monroe, work out some possible scenarios and oversee the other teams. I'll make some calls and work from a few angles I might be able to use. Right. Next meeting, tomorrow morning." Jac started stacking his paperwork. "Oh, and Rebecca, you do not leave out of sight or sound of Mark or Carter until further notice."

"I have work to do. I can't just sit at home and do nothing."

"Rebecca, if you need a spanking to settle, then that is between you and Carter, but I assure you that you will sit wherever Carter puts you, and you'll not complain. We are not taking any unnecessary risks with you."

"I never realized you were such a bully." Becky crossed her arms, and several men grunted and coughed while looking anywhere but at Becky.

Sharlee smiled and spoke sotto voce. "It's finally focused on you and not only me. Good luck."

Becky shrugged and shared a small grin.

"Do you need some of my attention, my dear?" Jac asked Sharlee.

"Nope. I'm just fine with my current ration of attention. Thanks." Becky giggled at Sharlee's response.

"If that changes, you *will* tell me." Sharlee didn't answer.

Jac turned back to Becky. "You can work from home if you want, and you can work on the inventory question with Jessie, think about other things that might have been missed the first hundred times you went back over them, and give us time to do our thing."

Becky's body language screamed, "No." But what she did say was, "Fine."

Jac raised his brow. "Excuse me?"

She looked at him with a sigh. "I get it. I'll work from home, but I don't know why it's safer there than here. Actually, I submit it isn't. Sir."

Callie nodded. "She has a point."

"Levi, go home with Carter and make some upgrades to their security."

"I've got as good as Kaden's system," said Carter.

Mark shook his head. "Come with me to the supply room, my friend. Let me show you what you really need."

"Okay, Becky, you can stay in the computer room with Sharlee and Kaden and give them some information about some of the key players, and then Carter can come and grab you when they are ready."

"But what about your phones and appointments, and assignments and..."

"Monroe, do you have your rubber paddle here?"

"Okay, okay. But you will be sorry I'm not there."

"I will miss you because you know everything about everything, including me, but I will not wish you were in the office where people expect you to be. You are special to all of us, and there is no discussion about keeping you safe. It will happen."

Garrett sent them off with an admonition. "No one goes anywhere or does anything iffy until they have cleared it with me. Have I made myself clear, ladies and gentlemen? No going rogue under any circumstances."

There were nods, but Carter knew that was lip service. It was Becky who needed protection, and they would do whatever it took to make that happen. He escorted Becky to the computer room.

"Feeling a little sassy today, I see," said Carter.

"Frustrated and unheard."

"Oh, baby, we hear you and understand that you are used to running everything from your command center, we depend on that and know whom to go to when we have a question about nearly anything, but it isn't safe. Someone knows your office's direct number from the outside. They got to you without going through the switchboard or our main line. That means it's closer than we first thought. And yes, unfortunately, that means that one of our people, present or past is threatening you. That can't happen. So, for now, you play by my rules."

"When is it ever any different?" she complained.

"Never when it concerns your safety, so buckle up and hang on because I'm driving this boat." He dropped a kiss on her lips and came back for another sweet taste. "Mmm, better get out of here before I embarrass myself and you."

"Why can't I ever stay mad with you?"

"Because you know I love you every minute of every day, and Daddy is always right."

Carter headed toward the basement and their security systems supply room, the adrenalin pumping.

The hunt was on.

Chapter 13

Karl sounded exasperated. "Let me show you. I borrowed some of James' space, and I know I didn't tell him, but he had an unused corner of the warehouse, so I borrowed it when I got a great deal on some items and ran out of storage on my half. Come down on the weekend, and I'll show you."

"The things that are said to be in the boxes couldn't be there, and they can't be as small as they say. And why are they in Dad's inventory?"

"Because they were counted with his."

"But there wasn't a line item created to put the stock alerting to whomever took the inventory that it did not have an invoice."

Karl hesitated. "Right, because it's my inventory."

"Fine but who counted it for Dad's? It was done intentionally. I have a forensic accountant looking at this, and she agrees with me. We took measurements and calculated what it could hold. Then we followed the invoices, and finally reviewed the count. The inventory that was too much wasn't new inventory. It was the exact same inventory, only more than was purchased. In other words, the items in the inventory weren't new or unidentified on the surface, like would have happened if you found a random good deal. No, this is fishy."

"How can that be? No, you're wrong."

"They seemed to be multiples of the same items only bought from someplace else or never bought at all because they have no invoices or payments to show the transaction ever happened, meaning it was a bad attempt at a cover up of some kind. I think something else could be in those boxes. They aren't as they are labeled or something."

"Because it was mine, for the store."

"Do you have the invoices to prove it?"

There was a long pause where Karl said nothing. "I must have them."

"So, what you're saying is that you bought from his suppliers, and you put it in his warehouse space instead of your own inventory space and no one noticed when counting things. And then, when it was pointed out, you allowed him to count it as part of his inventory. That's bad news for you and bad business for him, so why would you do that?"

"I needed it to appear that the business was doing better than it was, so I purchased inventory from my own accounts to sell from my store to boost my revenue on the books. I used the account I newly opened with James' distributors because their cost point is insignificant compared to others."

"You know what this looks like."

"I do. It looks like I'm somehow getting inventory under the table. I'll show you what is really going on. There are smaller boxes because they are small things for the cages and a few little things to send home with the animals, stones and so on. Exotic animals are pricier than people realize, and the markup isn't as much as you would think."

"But that means you are competing with Dad's business, and you contracted not to do that when Dad fronted the money for you to open your pet shop."

There was silence for a few moments. "I didn't think you knew that."

"Dad has told me everything because when he no longer runs things, I'll take it over but from a distance. You have a non-compete clause and you still haven't paid back his investment, despite having money for overflow backstock and a new house and car."

"I'm being honest when I say the business isn't doing as well as I had hoped."

Something didn't ring true. The car he drove was about fifty thousand dollars, and his house was new in the last five years.

"Then how do you make the payments on that car and your house?"

"Luckily, they are paid off."

"If your business isn't doing well, how can that even be?"

There was a silence that spoke volumes to Becky. "Just come this weekend. I'll show you."

"You have invoices and payment trails?"

"Of course. Just come."

Now he was sounding like he was becoming desperate for her to come. Becky knew Carter nor anyone else would let that happen. She would be getting her car back tomorrow with the information they gathered. Another meeting would be happening, and Becky wasn't sure if she should bring this up or not. She had already sent the results to her father's private email and the cloud. Now what?

Did she ask Jessie to work on this more or just leave it to the accountant? Becky had hoped that since Jessie couldn't do much in a day and certainly couldn't walk around as she had expected, helping her work on the accounting problem would lower her frustration and loneliness. But would it be too much to continue using her help? She called Jessie to discuss it.

"You don't know how much I love a problem to sink my teeth into. The others come by, but I worked on exciting projects before coming to Jac. Don't get me wrong, I'm happier than I've ever been, but sometimes I miss it. You have saved me from insanity, and I can't thank you enough. Now, let's plot our next course of action."

There was so much to untangle, and Becky remembered how crazy Mark had been when the love of his life got in the way of a government official and that official's efforts to step up to more prominent and higher positions. This wasn't nearly as big a deal, of course. And Becky was thankful that Jessie was anxious to join her in untangling the mess. It made it easier to manage.

Mark's agreement that it wouldn't hurt her to find out why there was such a difference in numbers made things more relaxed. The problem was, the deeper Jessie dug, the more obvious it had become. Something was illegal in this set up and she was afraid to discover who and what was involved. Now with her uncle's most recent call, it made more sense and yet it still wasn't right.

Becky started to withdraw, having a hard time knowing things were not on the up and up. And she wasn't working, not what she was used to and that depressed her mood more. She wasn't sleeping well or eating well despite her watch guard getting stern. Carter was careful to give her space and yet, not let her get into her own head for too long, but things were getting harder.

She decided to go back to her parents' home, but how to tell Carter was another story. She chose to stay home more and more until after two weeks and nothing else was discovered, she sent Jac her resignation.

"Since I can't come and do my full job, and there is no end to this seclusion with insufficient information to go forward, I am submitting my resignation. Effective immediately."

Becky watched Jac's name come up on her cell phone as he called her not a minute after she had emailed the note. She ignored the message, and it went to voice mail. Carter came into the office a couple of minutes later.

"Baby?"

"I'm not talking about it."

She pushed past him and left the room. Becky was under no illusion that if he wanted her to stop, he could have just filled the door, but he let her walk past him. It was obvious that even he thought maybe it was time to back up. He'd say he was doing what she wanted him to do, but she could see the handwriting on the wall.

Before, when she had a problem or something Carter couldn't easily work out, he would back up when she needed him to push forward. He would take the easy way out, the one that said he was just doing what she wanted. When, in reality, she wanted her Daddy, bold as brass, to tell her no and take over. When they went off bodyguard duty the first time, Carter backed off and gave her space. Not completely, but some. She didn't know how to handle that but now, it sucked.

A voice in the back of her mind told her to tell him. It was her responsibility to tell him if she wanted or didn't want something in their relationship, but she always had a hard time doing that. She could hear Carter in her head saying, "If you want to be heard, you have to make a noise."

It didn't matter. Becky was going to see her sister. The one who thought Becky had thrown her life away working as Jac's assistant. Actually, she called Becky his secretary, and said it was a degrading position. Trish didn't understand how much it meant to Becky to be at the center of everything that was going on in the building. Where everyone was, what their job was, and the strategies behind their assignments gave meaning to her position. Jac wanted her input, and he put stock in it. That said a lot considering the team's considerable experience. She didn't want to give that job up, but what else could she do? It wasn't fair to Jac.

She picked up her phone, entered the main bathroom and locked the door.

"Trish?"

"Becky? What's wrong?"

"Can I come and visit for a little bit? Just a couple of days. I need to breathe different air."

"Did that behemoth or his monster friends do something to you?"

"What? No, no, they're wonderful. I just need a little break, and I don't think I'm comfortable going to Mom and Dad's house right now."

"God, I heard. Someone tried to bomb your car?"

"Me! Someone tried to kill me, Trish!"

Her sister hadn't called her after that incident. She'd let things settle. While Becky tried to devise a viable excuse as to why her sister couldn't generate enough interest to check in on her only sibling, it was possible that she didn't think it was a real threat or maybe she wasn't in the country or something. Regardless, she would have broken the sound barrier to get to Trish if the tables were turned. It was time to admit that her sister was all about herself. Becky was biologically connected, but since she couldn't tell Trish what she did or that the company did more than security, Trish dismissed her as uninteresting. Boring. A waste of her time. And didn't that suck to have to admit that?

"Are you okay now?"

Becky did love her sister, though. "I'm good."

"Great. Sorry to rush away, but I have a date for an opening, and I can't be late. I don't want the play to start without me. Actually, you can't gain entrance to this thing after a certain time. Something about interrupting the creative flow. Whatever, so I have to go. We'll talk soon, okay?"

Becky sighed. "Okay. Love you."

"Love you too."

She disconnected the phone. Becky used to love her life, but right now, she almost hated it. She finally got Carter to admit why he was hesitant about kids and then agreed they could have children in the future. Now, this messed up bomb thing. It was likely a mistake, which is what Carter said, but she couldn't believe it. She didn't think he did either. Wrong house or wrong vehicle? Or the right house and wrong car? Becky stopped dead in her thoughts. That could mean they meant it for Mom or Dad. Whoever the hell "they" were. Or, the right vehicle, the right house, and she was the intended target. But why?

After thinking more about it, Becky decided she had to get back there. She had no choice but to determine whether it was for her or her parents, and then figure out why. Becky came barreling out of the bathroom and ran into the immovable wall named Carter.

"What is going on here? Did you send Jac a resignation letter? And what the hell, calling Trish and asking to stay with her for a few days?"

"Change of plans. I mean on where I'm going. Gotta go make sure my parents are okay and that no one is targeting them."

"Baby..."

She kept trying to get around him. He was always stopping her from doing things she wanted to do. Even as she thought it, she knew it wasn't true.

"Becky..."

"No. I'm not stopping. I have to check on them; they're my parents. I'll stay there until we figure this out."

"I had Jac call Nick Sharp, who is upgrading the security at your parents' house. It's going to be tested today. That's what brought me to look for you when I got that message from Jac about your resignation. That is something we will discuss after this system is synced in and tested. Then you can dial in at any time or stay tapped in at all times."

"I have to be there. I'm going. You don't get it. Your parents aren't in danger."

"Like hell you are." He swept her into his bulky arms and carried her over his shoulder, ass up and landing a flurry of damn hard slaps to her backside.

"Stop. Pickle juice!"

Carter stopped spanking her and rubbed her bottom until they were in the bedroom, where he laid her on the bed and sat beside her. "You safe-worded me. Why? What's wrong?"

"You don't listen to me. I tell you that I can't leave them exposed, unprotected. Trish is too busy. She wouldn't ever show up to help unless they were on their deathbed. She just doesn't think about other people, but I do. My mom and I might not always get along, but she's still my mom, and I can't let anything happen to her."

"I would never allow your parents harm if I could stop it. That's why we are doing this. In the same breath, I would never let you waltz into a situation that has already proven to be dangerous. You can't ask me to do that."

"You're a lot like the rest of them when it comes to what you think is right and what other people think is right. We try to conform and usually can meet in the middle, but when we can't, you bulldoze through. And I just don't want that right now. I don't know if I want that at all."

"You are my first priority, and I am not letting you out of my sight or hearing until this shit is found and cleaned up. Don't ask me to do it because I will have to deny you. I love you, but getting upset and going off half-cocked will not work. It isn't like you. You've dealt with things like this before. I know this is different because it's you and involves your parents, but we are already doing everything we can to keep everyone safe.

And that starts with you. So now it's time to tell me what new development you're focused on possibly harming your parents."

"That bomb might not have been aimed at me but to get to my dad. I know what I'm doing, and you have to get out of my way and let me do it. I might have been the one who brought it to their doorstep by discovering the discrepancy in accounting and inventory and that whole warehouse mess. If I had just taken their numbers and not gone back over as an extra measure, none of this might be happening."

"Or their accountant would have figured it out pretty quickly. Baby, we're also working on that angle, and if you hadn't thrown a frantic call of incoming, all hands on deck in the middle of all of this, you would have known that. Our meeting this morning, which you declined to attend and instead sat in the reception desk safe room, covered all that and more. You're going nowhere until I know what you know. Now talk."

"I know what I'm doing."

Carter crossed his bulky arms across his brawny chest and gave her the disapproving Daddy look. "Okay, convince me. Tell me what your plan is or tell me what you want to do."

Becky's fists clenched, her body tensing as her stubborn resistance fought against her better judgment. She had wanted him to be the man she fell in love with. She wanted him to get strong and stand up to her when necessary. And most often, when personal stressors threatened to overwhelm her, like now, she tried to fall into her pampered headspace. She craved yielding to him so he could take care of her. That was the woman that called to his Daddy Bear the strongest.

In the beginning, Becky hated to love their dynamic so much when he was in control. She loved her independence, but she hated it when it came to their relationship. Carter was always respectful but now that he no longer stood back and allowed her to do what she wanted, she fought back against the boundaries. But still, inside, she wanted him to hold fast the line.

In the last month or so, he had become a different man once they had figured out his hang-up about kids and had become the man that she had first fallen in love with. And that was all good, right? Her head said yes, and her heart agreed, but the old Becky said *hell no*.

Becky opened and closed her mouth several times like a fish out of water, the tears racing down her cheeks again. She knew he was watchful of her and could feel his disappointment when she squared her shoulders. She took a deep breath. Becky stared up at him like a stubborn teen, refusing to give up her sources.

"You safe-worded me so now you have a responsibility to talk to me."

She stared at him but said nothing.

"Baby, I want to know what you're thinking. It's obviously something heavy. Let me share it with you."

Becky didn't make a move. She just sat in stubborn mode.

"Or, we can start this party off with some honest-to-goodness discipline for attempting to go off the grid and risking yourself. Your decision."

Becky shivered as Carter dropped his shoulders in resignation and unbuckled his belt. From Carter's mannerisms, his grim expression, and the way he slowly slid the worn leather from his pant loops, allowing her to change the outcome, Becky knew he was in complete control. And whatever he was about to do, she knew she could stop him but wouldn't. She needed this to break through her barriers and her pain. Deep, raw need ate at her, and she needed him to take over. But she couldn't ask for it.

Becky craved his dominance to take away the image that she was in control so that she could let him handle this like he wanted to, like they both needed him to. She knew how precious she was to him; that was all she needed to know. Now was the time to let go, but she couldn't. He'd have to take back control. And just as she thought he would do the deed for them both, he dropped his hand from his buckle. No!

"Are you trying to manipulate me to do what you need but can't ask for?"

"I DON'T LIKE TO BE told what to do." She raked her hand across her face roughly. Her hot tears of frustration fell faster.

"I get that. I know you, even if you don't think I get you as well as I used to, but I do. I actually know you better. So now it's time to open up and tell me what's happening. You're sending up all these flares, and these SOS signals, and I tried to allow you to work some of it out yourself, but it's not having the desired effect. It's time I step in and take over. I will not let us slip apart because I was too afraid to rock the boat. We will have other things that shake us, but what are we doing if we can't come together and share the burden?"

Carter watched his baby cry silently. He needed to push the point. He knew it like he knew his own name and he wanted to be her Daddy, lover, and partner forever, but this was a turning point. His Waterloo. Likely one of many. He took a mental breath and forged ahead.

"Rebecca Shea Carrington, I love you with all that I am, but you're hurting inside. Tell me what's going on so we can fix it. I don't want to drag it out of you; I shouldn't have to, but I will. The thing you can't do is try to manipulate me to do what you need without using words."

Becky sniffed and brusquely ran her face across her arm. "It's fine. I'm fine. It's not a big deal. I just overreacted. Maybe I'm not getting enough sleep."

Fine. He loathed that word. He reached for his buckle again, knowing he would have to prove his love and dominance. Becky looked down at the floor and didn't meet his eyes. Carter knew that when she started searching the floor beneath her feet for answers, she wasn't being truthful. No choices left. Time to get stern.

It fucked with his gut whenever he unbuckled his belt and slipped it completely out of the loops for use on his baby's ass for things other than play. Still, if it took that to break through her wall of secrets and defenses to prove his love, the value he placed on her, their relationship, and most of all, to keep her safe, he would do it.

Steeling his face to the turmoil inside, Carter laid the belt on the bed and pointed to the spot between his thighs. "Right here, baby."

She surprised him by meekly going to that space, her head down, hands folded in front.

"You know I love you."

She nodded.

"Words, baby. Do you want to say your safe word now?"

She shook her head, and he released a grumble deep in his chest. "No, Carter, I don't want to say it."

"And what is it?"

"Pickle juice, but you're scaring me."

"Are you afraid of me, baby?" He almost stopped breathing.

Becky shook her head. "No, but you never ask me if I want to use my word or what it is."

"I have to be sure because you used it. I need to know that you understand that I will always honor it. If I start, I have to know you understand it's because you didn't ask me to stop. I can see the body language and the antsiness that you are desperate for me to take control, so you don't have to decide what to do right now. I'm going to do that."

"Okay. You know, I really love it when you Daddy me. I love you."

Carter almost stopped his hardass moves at that moment, but his mental kick in the butt told him to get his shit together and be the man she needed.

Leaning in, he kissed her lips deeply until she moaned her desire in his mouth. He released her lips and hooked his thumbs in her sweatpants, dragging them and her panties to her feet.

"Step."

She hesitated, and he waited her out. She stepped out and his hands went to her plump bottom cheeks, rubbing, squeezing, patting them. His manipulations became increasingly intense. Without another word, he pulled her over his thigh, placing her upper body over the bed, her legs dangling and her bottom well centered. Because he wanted her to feel him, and he needed to keep contact with her, he started with a sound hand spanking.

Swat. Swat. Swat. Swat.

Hard spanks in the same place got her immediate attention. She wasn't getting a warm-up because this spanking had a naughty, needy girl on the receiving end.

Swat. Swat. Swat. Swat.

Another four in the same spot on the other cheek. Then he covered her entire backside with deliberate spanks, meant to convey that Daddy is in control and minding him is very important to his baby's safety and welfare.

Becky rarely kicked or twisted during a spanking, but she also rarely experienced a punishment spanking. Now, her movements had become rhythmic. He stopped spanking and grabbed his belt. Rolling the well-worn leather around the buckle locked in his hand, he let the leather end land on her ass. She cried out. She knew she could use her word, but he also knew she wouldn't. He watched and would go nowhere close to her endurance line.

Thwap. Thwap. Thwap. Thwap.

He raised her so her sit spot and upper thighs were displayed better. Another five leather stripes on her quivering bottom were enough. She had cried herself out, and her resistance had gone as well. Now, they would get somewhere, and it would reassure her he was again her Daddy in every way.

The belt hit the floor, the buckle's brass jangle signaling the landing, but Becky didn't show any notice. Carter scooped her up and slid his body further on the bed, bringing Becky with him and placing his back against the headboard. Pulling her to him so he could cradle her in his arms, he drew her close and rocked until she was ready to speak.

"Sorry I was so stubborn. I just couldn't find a way out of my anger and frustration."

"How are those now?"

She shared with him a shy, silly smile. "Mostly gone."

"Good, now back to where we were. Tell me what is going on. What has changed the plans? How have the circumstances changed?"

"Okay, but don't interrupt me with your sage advice until I'm done telling. Promise?"

Carter raised his eyebrow in disbelief, but she was so damn cute in her best Daddy Bear's Baby Bear pampered headspace. He nodded. "Go on."

Becky stumbled and had a few false starts, but once she got going, everything came tumbling out. Her suspicions, thought processes, fears, the decision to go to her parents, and all the pent-up emotions associated with everything from the past weeks. And blessed tears. She was a mess for a while, but as she spilled all the jumbled chaos inside, things began to take shape and meaning for Carter.

How his girl could have kept so much from him was difficult to comprehend, but he knew it was partly because he had withdrawn from a deep connection for too long when he feared the marriage conversation. Now, that wasn't the case. Now he was deep diving into their relationship, taking charge, which had thrown his girl off track. Carter listened and responded when necessary but otherwise sat and held his baby as she spilled her pain all over him. He wanted it all out, so he didn't try to direct or ask any questions now. Just let her go until she was spent, and the words no longer flowed.

"I'm sorry, baby," he crooned as he resumed rocking her. "I left you stranded, and you felt you needed to deal with so many things alone. But I told you before, and I meant it then and now. You do not have to deal with things alone anymore. I was afraid to rock the boat, but this is Daddy rocking the boat hard. No more secrets, or there will be consequences. No more handling tough issues alone. No going off when I don't know where you are, the times you will be gone, or the mission that takes you there. And I'm going to keep you in the loop with whatever we find or don't find and work through the emotions attached together."

"You don't want all of this garbage, Carter. You want nice and easy, wrapped up with a bow."

"Not anymore. Your Daddy Dom is back and trying to hold the line. It's been hard with all of the changes and scares. I didn't want to be insensitive, but it seems I missed the mark on that. I hope I pushed the I'm in charge concept today. You will mind me, or you will find yourself in a pile of trouble.

"There will be consequences if you break the rules, and reddening your backside will be only one method. I'm re-initiating corner time, soap for talking bad about yourself or too coarse of language, lines for reinforcing the rules you broke and so much more. How does that sound?"

"Heavenly but not, at the same time. And I don't mind you. That's archaic."

"Use whatever word you want to use but you will follow the rules, and I'll make sure you float to heaven often. Now, let's work through this mess."

Chapter 14

"Rebecca, I don't care if you decide you don't want to work with us anymore. You are still part of my family, and I have a seating arrangement that works for me. You will respect me and sit in your assigned seat."

"Jac, I'm not your assistant anymore or a child on the school bus."

"The fuck? What do you mean you aren't his assistant?" asked Levi.

"I quit."

"However, I haven't accepted her resignation, and she is required to give me four weeks' notice. Even if I accept it, there will be four weeks after she comes back to the office that she will need to work through before she can actually walk away."

Garrett looked from Jac to Becky. "Yes, that's right. It's in her contract."

"Since when?" asked Becky.

"It's there," said Jac. "I expect you to honor your contract."

Becky's eyes narrowed as she glared at Jac. She knew what he was doing, but it wouldn't work. She would need extended time with her parents to keep them safe. "I want to see it."

"Later. Right now our IT department gurus will explain how your choice to go off-grid, alone, has contributed to your incidents."

Becky opened and closed her mouth a few times before closing it for good.

Mark, the sadist, leaned forward on the conference table. "Go ahead."

Kaden spared a glance in Sharlee's direction. She was strangely quiet as Kaden explained to everyone about the tracker. His voice gentled when he turned to Becky. They all knew Carter was her Daddy, but how that dynamic played out in her, and Carter's relationship was never so evident as when Carter had refused her to sit away from him.

When she had not moved, he picked her up and placed her in her seat. He didn't let his hand leave her thigh. It was vital that he knew where she was and what she was doing, like all the guys and their women, but Carter tried to pull her into his lap the moment they sat down.

The other men seemed to instinctively know that their women would blow a gasket if they violated their professional workplace space. Becky gave a mutinous glare and then wiggled in her seat. She was either sitting gingerly on a plug or spanking, or she was aroused, or all three. No one smiled but several looked away for a moment.

They listened as Kaden pointed out that these attacks could be crimes of opportunity, targeted, or accidents. "Take the snowbank incident. If she were being watched, it was a perfect situation to push the snow where it needed to go, but who would go there with a snowplow on their truck and use that vehicle for a deliberate crime."

"Someone who already knew what they were going to do," said Monroe.

"Yep. And knew where she was," added Levi. "But how would our friend know that Becky was at your place?"

Kaden nodded. "That is the piece that makes you wonder if it was an accident. The timing and the situation takes a crime of opportunity off the table."

Mark asked. "Who knew you were going out that night, Becky?"

"All of you. And my mom. I told her the ladies were going to let down their hair. She told me to take an Uber so I could drink." Becky shook her head. "And it wasn't my mom any more than it was any of you."

"And what about the vehicle incendiary device in the driveway?" asked Garrett.

"That might be a little harder to come up with anything but targeted."

"For someone, anyway," said Jac. "What is the likelihood of it being the wrong car?"

"Don't know. It wasn't sophisticated, so it could have been an internet special," said Mark.

"Fuck, there isn't anything we can do but wait," said Carter.

"That's why we need to flush whomever the fuck it is out," said Levi.

When she resisted, Carter tried to pull Becky into his lap again and said something into her ear. She stopped momentarily and nodded, sucking her lower lip between her teeth. As the conversation about strategies to draw out the culprit grew more intense, Carter became more restless and volatile. He pulled Becky to lean against his side when Levi suggested they let her go to her parents with bodyguards and security.

"I don't want her there. She could get hurt. No. It's not going to happen." Carter stood to pace but stopped and sat back down next to his girl. "There has to be another way, and we will find it, but Becky has already had two near-fatal attacks, and I will not purposely put her in the line of fire. They could be successful the third time around."

"Da-Carter, you'll keep me safe." Becky put her hands around his muscular, tensed bicep.

"No, Rebecca Shea, I will not have it. I don't know what kind of man you think I am, but I'm sure you know I would never allow you to do something to put yourself in harm's way. I spend all my time ensuring you're safe, healthy, and happy. No."

Becky's voice was clear and calm. And determined. "If this will end everything so we can go back to normal," she put her hand up to stay the response several wanted to make, "*our* normal, then I'm going to do it. I'd like you with me, but I can do it without you if necessary." She turned to Jac. "Tell me how this will all work."

CARTER FELT LIKE HE was losing his ever-loving mind. They had just gotten their relationship back into the pattern he and Becky enjoyed best, and this shit had to happen. As much as Carter was proud of his Becky offering to do the tough stuff so they might end this stand-off, he was in control. Or at least he thought he was, and maybe that was the problem.

As much as he supported the other women taking bold steps even when it was against their partner's desires, when it came to his own woman, he didn't handle that very well. In fact, he took it just as well as the other guys had when faced with letting their women do something that was outside the bounds of safety, even a little bit. Sharlee had done it. Jessie and the rest of the women had all put themselves out there to end whatever was the demon stopping them from living their best lives.

He sat back and reflected on how he understood the men but also supported the women over the last years. Now he knew how much of a hypocrite he actually was. Because the idea of letting Becky get out there and expose herself to one or more people who wanted to end her, possibly for the information they perceived her to have or that they knew she had, scared him mute.

Jac said that nothing would happen until they got the intel back from Nick Sharp's people, so until then, they'd wait. Carter figured they'd waited long enough for the research into people around there.

Jac leaned into Becky as she spoke quietly to him. He shook his head and answered close to her ear but loud enough for Carter to hear. "No, I didn't accept your resignation. No, you can't quit until this is all over and we have a long conversation. No, you can't come back to work until then, and that last question isn't something I can answer. That is a Carter question." Jac looked around the room. "And that does it for us today on this subject. Any old business?"

The room began to empty ten minutes later, and before long, only Carter and Becky were left. She stood, and the fingers that grasped her wrist stopped her from leaving.

"Carter, let me go."

"Sit down, Bec. This is important."

"I wanted to visit before everyone left."

"Understood. I'll take you to see them as soon as we are done. Remember that conversation we had after the snowplow incident? The one about you having some Little tendencies?"

"Yes."

"I'm getting a lot of those indicators recently. Your pampered mindset wants to be pampered more and I love that, but it makes you more vulnerable at times."

"Meaning you won't let me go in to help draw that someone out." Her whole face took on a pinched look.

"Meaning," he paused for effect, "there will be strong safeguards in place and plenty of back-up."

Becky looked up from her nails, her eyes full of excitement. "I can do it?"

"Tentatively. But if you get hurt, after you're healed, and the bad guys eliminated, I will paddle your ass nightly for a week. Hell, a month."

"Okay," she said with a big grin.

"Okay...?"

"Okay, Daddy."

Carter slid his hands up to either side of her face and she watched as he lowered his head to kiss her lips hard. Becky's moan grew as he drew back. "Can't do anything here, baby, so let's get your visiting out of the way so we can go home."

"M-kay."

Carter just smiled and shook his head. Yeah, his girl's pampered mindset was engaged, even if she wasn't comfortable with the knowledge or inclined to admit more than it resembled being a Little. It was just a label, and he was more interested in meeting her needs no matter what others wanted to call them. So long as she continued to allow him to push her limits and responded to his Daddy voice and rules, it all worked for him. He loved this woman.

Several days later, the invitation came, putting everyone on alert. Garrett said no outright, but Jac was still optimistic that Ramirez was not the one who had targeted Becky. He had a clear explanation as to why he said the things he'd said.

"It was impolite and bad business to have a conversation about one of my personal difficulties with my suppliers in your parking lot, but I was definitely not referring to you, Jac, or any of the others in your employ in the way you thought. I may have mentioned Jac and his team but that was in compliment only. Speaking derogatory to someone I wanted to do business with would have been the height of stupidity, and while I was indiscreet, I am not stupid."

Jacquard and Associates stood to gain a number of very lucrative clients. Jac had entered into the contract with Ramirez, and it had been mutually beneficial so far. There had been no surprises, and his people were treated well. Besides, the best thing to do was keep a close eye on him; this was the easiest way. Being a bodyguard and monitoring security for Ramirez's group put Jac in control. Just where he wanted to be.

Becky accepted the man's explanation, but she didn't believe it, not totally. But Jac and Garrett agreed that Garrett would have oversight of that contract because it would keep the contact at a minimum and, therefore, out of Becky's office.

When Jac said that Ramirez was inviting Garrett's team to his observation floor to watch the winter boat parade from his business' balcony overlooking the river, Carter declined out of hand.

"Thanks for the invite, but we aren't going. I still don't trust him as well as you do, Jac."

"Trust isn't the question, because we are always guarded but there are some things I don't worry about and that is being attacked while standing next to him."

The next day, Monroe called Carter. "I understand why you said you don't want to go to Ramirez's place, but what better opportunity will we get to case the joint and figure out if he is hiding anything we need to know about?"

"Not with Becky."

Monroe sighed loudly. "Don't get so dominant you forget how to be open. That's a sure way to go down the wrong road in a relationship. You can only afford to make all the decisions with Becky's input. Consent is still the foundation of our lifestyle. Talk with her and see what she says."

Carter was afraid of what she would say, but Monroe was right. He needed to give her the opportunity to make up her own mind. Not that she would ever go alone, and he still didn't want her there at all, but agreement was important. Later that afternoon, he asked her.

"Carter," he raised his eyebrows, "Daddy, if he isn't the person doing these things, then I want to prove it, and this might help, but if he is, it might draw him out."

"Baby, in the middle of a bunch of Jac's crew? Not likely to draw him out."

"Maybe, but don't we have to try?"

Carter rubbed his hand over his forehead and into his hair. "I don't want to do it, don't want you there."

"But you will, right? We can go?"

The squeal that Becky released made Carter want to grumble and smile. He loved it when she was excited but hated that it was because of this issue. He was going to be concentrating on her the whole time. He prayed the boat show was short this year.

SHARLEE AND JAC DECIDED to bring Storm to the boat parade, and Finley came with them. Finley always accompanied Storm, but they and Ryker chose to watch from the inside, not the balcony. Finley's standing orders were to protect Storm at all costs, and she would use all of her Marine training to do just that. Finley was briefed on how to get into the off-site designated safe rooms that were now equipped to add a toddler. Everyone but Storm was keeping vigilance over the situation.

Callie and Mallory were on Ivy's boat being used by a local charity. Kaden was one of the judges, and since the boat was Ivy's, she was captaining. Leaving the four of them on the water or the dock, Monroe and Garrett were positioned to watch where Becky and Carter were standing. Carter had tried to get Becky to watch from the inside windows, but Ramirez had insisted she watch from the better view on the balcony. Many others were invited and milling about inside and out.

Levi had the weekend off to take care of a bit of family business, but Ryker came for extra protection. His military legal career spanned twenty-one badass years. His civilian legal career made him highly sought after. Jac hired Ryker the minute Jac and Garrett agreed to start the business, and they were good friends. The men may have respectable businesses now, but they could still take down the enemy without breaking a sweat.

Jessie and Mark stayed home due to her bed rest. Not long after the group arrived at the modern glass and steel industrial building facing the river, Carter wanted to leave. He wasn't impressed with the structure or Ramirez. Three men surrounded the businessman and Becky as Ramirez approached her.

"Miss Carrington, I am so sorry to have heard of your recent mishap. I have offered my services to your boss if you need any assistance in discovering what happened, and I now offer that to you." He looked at Carter and then back at her. "Were you mine, I'd be burning down the town looking for the culprit." Ramirez took a measured look around him, "I know your friends are doing the same. I am at your service."

Becky wasn't sure what to say, but it needed to be appropriate. "Thank you for your offer. I'm sure Jac will be in touch if that need ever arises." Ramirez walked off to another part of the room. Becky accepted a bottle of water graciously opened by the server before moving closer to the center-left of the group. She absently uncapped the bottle, taking a healthy drink. Ugh, a little bitter. She made a face. It tasted a little different, but it might have been the brand. She was unfamiliar with it. Recapping the bottle, she looked for her friends' boat to pass in front of them on the river.

When Callie and Mallory waved from Ivy's decorated vessel, Becky and the men waved back and cheered for them. The music from the float ahead of them was loud, and Becky felt herself being jostled forward hard. She was nauseous and her head felt heavy. She could feel herself being literally heaved up over the rail. The pressure was already gone when she had the wherewithal to yell, leaving her top heavy over the reinforced fencing. Then she screamed. Suddenly her legs were grasped by steel hands, and her waist was wrapped in the bulky arms of another.

"Go limp, Bec."

She did. Within the blink of an eye, she was against the door to the balcony and inside, where warm air accosted her cold limbs. The look she gave Carter must have conveyed her terror because he carried her to a sofa in the corner of the room and held her almost too tight to allow breathing, but it was what she needed.

"Go, go, go!" she heard Jac yell, and suddenly Becky was being rushed from the room in confusion.

Chapter 15

"Go. Go. Go!" said Jac. "Charlotte, haul your ass out of here. Send a message to Kaden and Callie once you are clear of this building. Tell them we are en route to Papa Bear's house. There is a mandatory regroup."

"What the fuck happened?" Jac asked over the melee that followed. It appeared to be more confusion than fear. "Never mind. Exit the building. Regroup once we are all out."

Becky looked around, and evidently, Ryker and Finley had already whisked Storm out of the building on their way home. Sharlee had closed her tablet and was headed for the door. Carter still had Becky in tow but was joined by Sharlee. Now they were flanked by Garrett, Monroe, and Jac. Becky was rushed out to the stairs along with Sharlee, as Carter led the way.

The vehicles had been parked close on purpose, and now it played out in their favor. Then Becky slowed and vomited on the ground.

Carter reached for the water bottle in her purse and uncapped it. "Here, take a sip of this."

"No, it doesn't taste right."

"Fuck." Garrett pulled out a bag he had in his inside pocket for some odd reason and took the bottle from Carter and recapped it. "Need to have this tested and fingerprinted. Let's hope we have a set after ours are eliminated." Garret took a fresh bottle from the back of his SUV and tossed it to Carter. "Get in. Let's get out of here."

Once everyone reassembled, Jac fielded a message from Ramirez, who had been calling for the last fifteen minutes.

"Reynaud." He nodded to whatever Ramirez said. "I haven't had a chance to find out all the details. I assume that Ms. Carrington was the only target." He listened. "That would be greatly appreciated. Right. I'll let you know."

"Cut his off, Jac," said a furious Carter, who was holding Becky in his arms in the corner of a large sofa in the operations room of Jac's home.

"It is my first thought, as well, but something doesn't seem right." Jac walked over to Sharlee and murmured something to her. She nodded, and he dropped a lingering kiss on the top of her head before continuing. "Charlotte will continue to work on the CCTV. Now, what else?"

"Her water may have been tampered with," said Garrett.

Becky whimpered, and Carter pulled her tighter to himself and spoke to her quietly.

Sharlee updated everyone. "Kaden will be on his way after he rates the last boat. Should be here in about twenty minutes. Callie said as soon as they hit the dock, she and Mallory will be on their way. Ivy has to finish emptying the boat of passengers before she can get here."

Monroe spoke up. "Mark is monitoring the situation from there, but if you need him, he says he will be here."

Carter shook his head. "No, he needs to stay with Jessie when he can." There were murmurs of agreement. She was too close to delivery to leave alone much.

"Levi says the same. He hasn't finished his family business, but he will cut it short if needed," said Finley as she entered the room with the baby monitor. "Storm went right to sleep." Sharlee tapped into the video feed from his room to a corner of one of her monitors.

Ryker strode in behind Finley, sitting next to her. The fact that Finley, who was a prior Marine, allowed him that luxury, spoke loudly. Carter wondered if Jac was paying attention to those two. Especially since Levi had been sniffing around the same badass nanny.

Attorneys were great for many things, but busting heads wasn't often one of their talents. Ryker trained with the 82nd Airborne Division and, as a civilian, with Jac's crew. He could definitely hold his own in hand-to-hand combat or a gunfight. However, in a courtroom, he could annihilate the opposition and walk away without a scratch. He preferred those types of encounters now he was forty.

Becky seemed to be in a better headspace to discuss the incident by the time Kaden and the girls showed up.

Jac turned to Becky. "Okay, we're all here with Mark on the phone. Levi is in another family meeting and will join if he can. What do you remember about the incident?"

Carter's arms rested around her for security and support while Becky rearranged herself in his lap. "Baby," he whispered, "have some mercy."

Becky grinned. "Sorry, Daddy," she whispered. "Now," she said in a louder, firmer voice, "First, the water. It just tasted funny to me. It could be the brand. I've never had that kind before. Anyway, the server who brought it simply handed it to me. It wasn't on a tray with others, just a single bottle."

"Odd because I was served a bottle from a tray, and I chose the one I drank. Was your bottle already opened?"

"No. He opened it right in front of me though, and I heard the little plastic connectors break, so it must have been closed."

"Or he did that to take the suspicion away from the bottle," said Callie, who sat beside Garrett.

"Probably," agreed Garrett grimly. "Anyway, I'll get this to the lab and see what we can get from the bottle."

Jac nodded. "Good. Go on, Rebecca. What else do you remember?"

"Nothing until I saw Ivy's boat. Callie and Mallory were waving. I yelled and waved back, then got a little dizzy, and nauseous. Then someone was pushing and shoving me up until I was on the railing. I screamed and was pulled down. I was still dizzy, but everything was moving anyway. Carter was pushing me out of the room, and you all know the rest."

"And when she got outside, she puked," added Monroe.

"Yeah, sorry about that, guys."

"I think it was the water," said Carter.

Becky nodded. "Me too."

Sharlee spoke up. "Okay, we have the footage before and after the incident from when Carter brought Becky to where we were."

Jac walked closer to the projected picture on the wall. "Run it backward. That's the main focus for now."

Sharlee or Kaden put it up on the screen, and everyone watched things happen backward, then forward, having it stopped to see specific parts slowly and then they reran through it again.

Ryker grumbled. "I hate this kind of surveillance camera. It pans. Fucking irritating."

"Right, but if it was one of the normal staff, wouldn't they know that? I mean, we can see who brought her the water. If you worked there regularly, you would know how the cameras worked and could avoid being caught."

Mallory had a point. Monroe followed up. "That stands to reason, so if we go on that premise, this wasn't a regular staff member, it is less likely to be Ramirez. Did he hire from outside to help serve?"

"Rebecca, keep notes." The room went still. "Fuck. Sorry. I've done things a certain way for so long that I go on autopilot. Charlotte, will you please write down the issues to follow up on?" Becky frowned but said nothing.

Sharlee stared at her husband. "Do you want to run the program, then?"

"Point taken. That's why we all need to stay in our place."

Monroe raised his hand. "I gotcha, Jac." He turned on the recorder on his phone, placed it in the center of the table and sat back.

Kaden continued. "Now, right here, it looks like when the girls were passing by because our people are cheering and waving, but then it pans again, and we miss the rest of the shot." Kaden leaned back in his chair.

"Sharlee, see if they could have gotten more at that moment. Another camera, maybe."

Mark swore as he watched from his screen at home. "Who put in this panning security system?"

Kaden spoke up. "I believe Levi, and I did. It can run continuously, and that is how we left it, but it has the option to pan only."

"So," asked Carter, "can we assume this was tampered with to put on sweep deliberately for this event?"

"Possibly," said Kaden.

"We can see who gave her the bottle but only the back of his head. He lowered his head when he left the deck. So does that mean he knows the camera is there or figures this is a high-profile man giving the party, so there must be cameras?" Monroe leaned back in his chair and rubbed Mallory's thigh.

"Another good point," said Garrett.

"And why did we not think Ramirez had nothing to do with this?" asked Carter.

Jac turned to him. "We can't be certain yet, but the evidence doesn't point that way. He's a shrewd businessman. He wouldn't do that in his own house. Honestly, Becky only heard his side of the conversation and not all of that. It just isn't enough, guys. Besides, Ramirez wasn't sure what had happened. Just heard yelling, then screaming, then a rush and scramble. In fact, many people didn't have any idea anything had happened. I know the guy isn't always above board, but he wouldn't piss in his drinking water, either."

It was quiet momentarily before Becky said, "I think you're right."

"Me too," said Ryker. "That begs the question, who wants to shut you up, Becky?"

Carter's face tightened. Becky answered. "My uncle."

The CCTV was removed from the screen, and a photo of Becky's Uncle Karl appeared in front of a warehouse. Becky went on to tell about the phone call a week ago that made her think it might be him.

"And that is why I have to go to my parents' house. I have to figure out how to fix this and watch out for them."

Monroe, the only other Daddy besides Carter in a room of Doms, said, "That will not be happening, Little girl. You will not go anywhere alone. We have already said that, and I have no doubt Carter has also made that very clear."

"But you don't understand. I have to do something to keep them safe. I have to fix this mess."

Finley, who usually stayed quiet, said, "Jessie is a forensic accountant, right? I bet she would be able to help you."

"She has. That's why I know my first concern is a real one."

"Okay, then Ryker tells me he is a good attorney." She paused to smile at him as he acted as though he was wounded by her wording of his prowess. "He might be able to help fix this."

"Possibly," said Ryker. "If something illegal happens in the business, we can stop it legally."

"But I have to be with my parents. I don't even care about the rest of this."

Jac sat next to Becky. "Rebecca, listen to this action plan and see if it won't work. Right now, we get notifications if anyone is coming onto or leaving the property at your parents' house."

"Your dad gave us permission, I promise," added Sharlee. Becky nodded.

Jac continued. "And then, we have Nick Sharp tagged into the feed, so if we need assistance or miss something, they will see it and respond. Until we get our ducks in a row, we'll do what we need to. But it will likely involve you."

"No problem."

Carter ran his hand through his hair. "With lots of back-up."

"Of course. I'm not putting my best personal assistant in jeopardy."

"I'm the only one you've ever had."

"There is that. See, the best." He smiled, and Becky groaned.

"Okay, keeping Becky and Carter here for now. The rest, go home. Bring me your ideas on going forward tomorrow at nine a.m."

THE FOLLOWING DAY THERE was energy around the conference table. Jac and Sharlee had yet to arrive, but Garrett wanted to get things going.

"Listen up. I know we are fewer today, but Levi will be back tomorrow, and Mark can join us because Jessie is officially off of complete bedrest and is on modified bedrest for another week." Garrett turned to Mark and slapped him on the back. "Great news, man. Give her our best. Won't be long now." Mark smiled, then groaned.

"Now, Becky has agreed to go in with escort and protection, and while he is doing it under protest, Carter isn't going to put up a fuss. Now, we can't go in there, guns blazing, so I think if Callie goes in with those two, we will get a better outcome. Callie can go anywhere Becky can. She can also seem like just a girlfriend and therefore not a threat."

"My superpower." Callie laughed.

Jac walked in. "It helps when we have a female operative in the field. It isn't anything we have ever had before. We have Charlotte, but she is not allowed in the field." He gave his wife a telling look.

"But she's kickass on the web," said Kaden.

"That she is." He paused. "We were late because we went to Ramirez and got his video. We watched it once with him, and he didn't know who the server was, so he gave us a list of the people yesterday, highlighting the temps for the day."

Sharlee nodded. "It's not him, but it might be someone that he has done some business with or something. They could have accessed the party through an invitation. It's a perfect blend-in. We've done it a few times ourselves. He won't give his sources or clients, but he will look at our key list of suspects to see if any of them are his people."

"Well, if that's the best we can do, then we'll take it. Once I know if anyone is on there, I'll know how to get the ground plan lined out. Carter, you'll give me a hand. We can do it over the secure IP."

"Sounds good," agreed Carter.

"Wait, what am I going to do?" Becky seemed out of sorts. She usually had plenty to do, but since it was her problem, she was out of the loop.

Callie spoke up. "You need to sound your parents out about having a couple of guests."

"Okay, I can do that, but do we have an idea when?"

"This week," said Callie. "As soon as tomorrow."

ARRIVING IN THE EVENING in Oak Ridge, Tennessee, was fascinating. It was a town of about 30,000 people, about a tenth of Lexington, and seemed so rural next to home. The lights gave off a small-town glow in a central area and then there were neighborhoods out around the center. Most people remember her town from the Manhattan Project. Becky had loved growing up there, but she loved her home in Kentucky, too.

Her mom had always hoped to do more than live in a small town like Oak Ridge. She'd tried to live vicariously through Becky in Chicago until Becky decided she didn't want fame and fortune or even a high-paying, stiffly professional job. She loved what she did and the people she did it with. And the pay was better than she had a hope of making in Chicago. Isn't that what life was all about? Trish didn't let her family into her life very often so Candace did the best she could in Tennessee.

Becky's mother fussed over the girls and left Carter to her husband. She still hadn't bought the whole security job being a viable career to support a wife and children on. She was convinced, despite Becky telling her otherwise, that her daughter was supporting the couple. James thought something wasn't quite right, but he was beginning to stay fuzzy longer during the day and didn't dwell on any one subject long.

The following day, after breakfast, Becky was encouraged to go down memory lane with her parents, discussing the early days of the animal supply business. They moved on to the warehouse, her Uncle Karl, and more. Callie played Becky's friend really well because, well, they were friends.

Later in the late morning, Becky offered to give Carter and Callie a tour of the community. "Carter has been here before, but Callie hasn't so I have some cool things to show you."

Candace shared some places she thought would be interesting and let the group of three go on their way. Once out of the house, they begin to investigate every part of Becky's family's life and the people in it, ending up at her Uncle Karl's store.

"Hi, Bobby. Where is Uncle Karl?"

"Oh, hi, Becky. Sorry I missed you the other week."

"Hey, sorry we didn't get a chance to talk. This is my fiancé Carter and my friend Callie."

He reached out to shake hands. "I didn't know you were coming in. Karl is at the warehouse, awaiting a delivery."

"Oh, I thought Monty did all of those."

"He used to, but he and Karl haven't been getting on that well lately. They had an argument or something." He shrugged his shoulders. "Anyway, I have to get back to work. Karl has been kind of cranky these days. You know how he can get."

She smiled. "I do. Nice to chat with you. See you later."

"Bye. Nice to meet you, Callie."

Once outside, Becky giggled. "Wow, you made an impression."

Callie rolled her eyes when Carter, who had been rather solemn since they left home, broke a slight smile.

"He's got to be what? Twenty? I am not into potty training my men."

Becky laughed. "So, it's men, is it? Does Garrett know?"

"Shut it."

Carter, who had finished with the ribbing, grew serious again. "It's getting late, so I vote we go grab takeout and go back to the Carrington's and eat. We can send the information we've gotten to Sharlee and see if any of it goes with anything else."

"Fine, but no takeout. My mom will simply be mortified. Let me call her and ask if she needs anything from the store."

They stopped for a bottle of wine and a six-pack of beer and enjoyed a hearty home-cooked meal of pot roast with all the fixings and apple pie. They relaxed in the evening, talking like they were there for nothing more than a visit. James seemed to grow fuzzier as the evening progressed. His memory and concentration diminished enough to feed Becky's fear that something like Sundowners Syndrome for early dementia was beginning. She mentioned it.

"How long have you been feeling fuzzy, Dad?"

Her mom answered. "I'd say about four months or so. Around Thanksgiving. When he thought something was going on at the store."

"Did I?" James laughed. "It must've not been important. Nothing happened."

"Do you remember what that was, Mom?"

"No, I don't pay that much attention to the business side of things. You know that."

"No, but I don't want you to go jumping in where you don't need to be," said James. "It's caused too much trouble as it is."

"Like what?" pushed Becky.

"Like Karl and Monty are barely talking anymore. Just turn in your paperwork to the accountant and let it go."

"Okay, Dad. Don't get upset."

"I'm not, honey. I'm just tired. I'll see you all tomorrow."

Becky looked at Callie and Carter and then offered to help her mom with the clean-up.

"No, I'm really all done. You go to your rooms or watch a movie in the den, and I'll see you tomorrow."

The next day, after breakfast, James left for work, forgetting his thermos. "Hey, we'll run it to him, so he has it for his morning coffee break."

"Thank you, dear. You know he loves his coffee."

"I do. Hey, what are you up to today?"

"Me? Same old stuff, but I have some errands in town this afternoon. I'm meeting a friend for lunch, but don't you worry, I'll be home in plenty of time to cook dinner."

"Mrs. Carrington are you sure you don't want me to grab something for us in town?" asked Carter.

"What? Absolutely not. We cook dinner around here."

"Yes, ma'am. How about our last night here? We will go out to dinner, my treat."

"Well, I'm not sure... If you can't afford it..."

"Mom, of course he can afford it. Would you quit? Now, dinner. You love that little Mexican place. Is it still open?"

"Mamacita's? It is. I love it; we haven't been there in almost a year. Carter, I think that would be very nice. Thank you."

"Okay. Great! It's a date. Do I need to make reservations?"

Candace blushed. "No. It's not fancy. Don't forget your father's thermos, Becky. I'm going to get ready. See you all later."

"Right. See you later, Mom." Candace went upstairs, and they headed out to the pet supply store. "She seemed preoccupied but maybe it's just me seeing things that aren't there."

"We don't brush off any feelings. We add it to the intel," said Carter.

After talking to her father's clerk, she left the thermos at his store and searched for her uncle with no luck. Then they head-

ed to look for Karl at his house, but he and her aunt had separated. So, if his car was gone, there would be no one home.
Becky tried to call him, but it went to voicemail.

"Where could they be?" asked a stumped Becky.

"Call Monty at the warehouse," said Callie.

"I have, but so far, no luck." "Okay, well, let me call to see if
we can go to the accountant's office now." Becky ended the call
and shook her head. "No luck. He is out of the office until tomorrow. I don't know that there is anything to do. Has Sharlee
or Kaden found anything?"

"I'll check," said Callie. Soon she put her cell back in her
pocket and shook her head. "They are waiting on some follow
up information and will call us with it as soon as they can."

"Well, it's twelve-thirty, and even if I haven't done much,
I'm hungry," said Carter.

"Of course, you are, big guy. Let's go to a little hole-in-the-
wall place with great lunch specials." Callie and Becky laughed.

The trio walked into the cute diner and looked at the well-
worn fifties café décor. Becky and Carter grabbed a table as
Callie headed to the ladies' room. When Callie exited, she
scanned the room to get reoriented to where Becky and Carter
were seated. Callie saw a woman that looked very much like
Mrs. Carrington leave behind a man that seemed familiar but
not James.

"Becky, was that your mom walking out of here a second
ago?"

Becky stood and looked out the front window. "It is. And
who is that with her? Monty? Monty is her lunch date?" She
watched the two hug and have a quick kiss before Candace

looked around and quickly slid into her car. Monty strode to his pickup and drove off in a different direction from Candace.

"I bet they went to school together," offered Carter.

"He didn't grow up here. He took the job with Dad right after he moved here about five years ago."

Callie said, "Don't jump to conclusions. It's the worst. Remember what Garrett and I went through? Don't repeat that mistake to any degree. Get proof first."

Carter nodded. "I agree, Bec. Either leave it alone or ask her directly."

"Carter, I can't leave it alone."

He sighed. "Then Callie is right. Go to her and ask. Don't guess because there are huge implications in other people's lives if you aren't careful."

They ordered, but Becky didn't eat much. Carter tried his Daddy move to get her to take a few more bites, but she wouldn't budge. Carter knew when Becky was to this stage of no return, he needed to leave her be. Nothing would progress in their investigation or her relationship with her mom until she knew the facts.

Becky wasn't one of those emotional eaters. Carter was. He ate his large meal and the rest of Becky's. Damn, he would need to work out to get rid of the extra calories and energy. Maybe he could go for a run. Take Becky with him. Callie probably needed a run, too. They'd go together. Yeah, that was a good idea.

"Let's try the warehouse again. Then I want to go home to have a conversation."

As they walked up to the warehouse, a large truck was unloading small boxes marked rodent food.

Carter stared for a moment and shrugged. "Huh, I used to have all kinds of rodents, and the food usually came in a box or bag, not small squares like that."

Callie said, "That tells me to follow the boxes."

"That's what it tells me, too. Bec, with me. I don't want you to wander off unprotected."

"This is my dad's warehouse, Carter."

"And you are the body we are guarding, remember? I let you come with the agreement that you would follow directions. We can go home now if you like."

His raised eyebrow did the trick. Becky fidgeted and then nodded. "Meanie."

"Whatever it takes, Baby Bear."

Callie's phone rang. "It's Sharlee. I'll follow you two in a moment. Let's get her intel."

Carter dropped a kiss on Becky's lips. His index finger lifted her chin to see his serious expression. "Is this getting too much for you, baby?"

She sighed. "No. I just have to figure things out. Something isn't adding up."

"We'll piece things together. I promise."

She nodded. "I know. Thanks for being here with me."

"No place else I'd rather be, baby. Now, let's see what's this new rat food." Carter opened the door.

The warehouse was busy with two men unloading stock and another putting it on the shelves. "Wow, I've never seen delivery people put the stock away. I mean, not ever."

Carter stayed quiet but kept his arm around her shoulders as they walked deeper into the space filled with fully stocked shelves.

"Hey, why are you stocking animal food on these shelves? This section is for store supplies. Food and supplies go three rows over and beyond. Uncle Karl doesn't use this much food for his rodents."

"Karl? I don't know who that is. This stuff is for Monty Rasher in care of Oak Ridge Animal Shop at this address."

Chapter 16

"Who is receiving this shipment?" asked Carter.

"Monty already signed for it and said just to leave it on the shelves."

Fuck. This situation was FUBAR and going south fast. Carter had to get his girl out of there because if those boxes held what he feared was in them, they all needed to get out. Fast. And if it wasn't one thing, it was likely another, and she didn't need to be mixed up with illegal drug shipments.

His urgency made a difference to Becky because she nodded and kept walking. Things to make a bomb or incendiary devices? Maybe they prepared them to be used. Was her Uncle Karl in on this, and that was why he was trying to sideline Becky? Or Monty? Things were adding up so fast they weren't. Too many dangers and variables to allow his girl to be in the middle.

He grabbed his phone and started talking to Kaden low and fast while walking Becky out.

"Hold on, Kaden." He turned to Becky. "There is shit going on here that we have to take a step back from and regroup. This may be more than Jac's standard clusterfuck. I hate when we have to bring in the local law enforcement but looks like that's what's going to happen."

He signed off with Kaden and began looking for Callie. Where the hell did she go? Carter's gut sounded off, and that wasn't good. He kept a lookout for Callie and walked his girl outside. As they exited the building, Carter saw his partner a distance off, talking on her cell and pacing.

Carter gave her a side nod to indicate they were heading for the car, and she nodded understanding. The explosive sound of a bullet as it ricocheted off the side of the reinforced steel bar on the side of the building and hit the top of his SUV had Carter yelling as he dove over Becky.

"Shh. I'm sorry, but you have to crawl under the car."

"But..."

"Do it!"

He watched a second longer to ensure she followed orders, then took cover on the other side of the car, leaving the doors open as extra protection. He opened the back door to let Becky roll under the undercarriage of the vehicle and then try to crawl into the front seat between the driver's side doors. Another shot rang out, hitting his side mirror. Becky screamed. Fuck, that was too close for comfort. A third shot hit the back wind-shield, exiting the front windshield. Becky screamed again.

"Fuck! Are you okay?" he asked with his gun drawn and searching where the shooter was staged. "Becky?"

"I'm okay."

"Stay down, baby. Don't move."

He stayed low, which was challenging for a big man. He wasn't used to being shot at in the middle of the day, but he studied the area where the shots seemed to originate from and located a slight movement.

The delivery truck drove off between the shooter and them giving Carter enough time to pull Becky to him and then down in front of the car. As soon as it was past him, another shot rang out, and this time he saw the flash before it hit the ground aimed at the undercarriage. It pinged off metal. There was answering fire. One gunshot rang out from behind Carter to the right, and he knew it was Callie as soon as he heard a blessed yelp of pain and the clatter of gunmetal hitting the ground.

As the shooter fell into view, Callie followed up with one that nicked the shooter's ear. They both began to walk to the writhing man on the ground. Carter kicked the gun far away, and Callie scanned the area before holstering her piece and pulling out the zip ties.

Becky was not moving from her place in front of the car, and it took a little convincing before she moved away and into his arms. Holding her out, he searched every bit of her body as the police sirens drew closer.

"Are you hurt? You're bleeding." He frantically looked for the wound.

"No. It's road rash. That's it, Carter. I'm okay. Just hold me."

Carter held her close as Callie sauntered up to them. Carter looked at the woman appreciatively. "That was a helluva shot. Thanks for having my six. I couldn't see where he was to get off a good round."

"Yeah, but I have to say, I expected a small town to be more friendly."

Carter chuckled. "You'd think."

The police checked the place out and brought in the paramedics, but Carter shielded Becky from seeing that. He worried it was her dad. But within a few minutes, James showed up and then Monty from somewhere undetermined, but still no Karl. When the police came out and spoke to James, they confirmed his brother had been wounded but not fatally. After a cursory look at Becky and confirmation only Karl and the shooter were injured, the ambulances left, each with a patient. Then came the fun part.

After long hours in which their stories were repeated more times than they cared to count, Garrett and Monroe arrived. Callie looked relieved to see her guy, and Monroe looked relieved everyone was okay. Guns were kept for ballistics. Nick Sharp, who ran with this police force, vouched for them as well as James. Garrett was able to call in a favor from the Lexington police force to get back up from them. That seemed to put them over the confidence line, and the police let them go.

They'd found the gun, impounded the shot-up vehicle, and the warehouse was closed until their forensics team and investigators were done with it. Oddly, that little bit of information on the warehouse closure seemed to rattle Monty. That and the fact that Becky was staring hard at his white truck.

"You'll get back to work in no time," said James.

Monty blew him off and tried to laugh, but it fell flat. "Did they say they found a gun in the brush?"

"Well, they'd have to because we didn't shoot at ourselves," Carter said dryly.

"Oh, right. Right. I just didn't process that bit of information, I guess."

They were all released together, and Garrett slept in Callie's room, leaving the den pull-out sofa for Monroe. Sleep was simply a word. And James didn't seem so scattered tonight.

"Hey, Dad. Did you ever get the thermos I left you at the shop?"

"No, I never did make it into the shop today. Too much work to do at the trade show."

"That's where you were all day?"

"Yes, didn't your mother tell you?"

"No, she didn't."

"Must have slipped her mind. I know what that feels like."

Carter stopped Becky from asking her mom about it later that evening. "Hush, baby, and let me think about this first. We have to figure a few things out and have a meeting tomorrow morning before we go opening any more cans of worms."

"Fiiine." She whispered back harshly.

Damn, Carter hated that word.

BECKY, CARTER, AND Callie were on Garrett's computer in a hotel room. They had decided that it was too many people in Becky's family home even though it did accommodate them well. Monroe took the room and the two couples stayed in the house. It gave Monroe the ability to wander as he needed to, undetected.

Sharlee seemed bursting with news and began talking as soon as things had settled down.

"Becky, did you see that truck? The white one that Monty drove up in?"

"I was looking at it but there was so much going on yesterday, I couldn't remember why it was so significant at the time and then I forgot. Oh my God. That's the truck. I know it is.

I knew it pricked my memory somehow, but I thought I was mistaken."

Kaden put the picture on the digital board. "Right. Now we found who the shooter was thanks to Callie's photos while waiting for the police. Royce Morton."

A picture of a male mid-twenties appeared next to Monty. "That's Bobby Morton's older brother. My Uncle Karl's part-timer."

There was nothing but shuffling papers for a few seconds before Garrett said, "Well, Karl was shot, so if it isn't Karl, and the truck belongs to Monty, but Monty wasn't there at the time of the shooting, and the shooter was Karl's clerk's brother, then who the hell has done what to make the inventory the key to everything? Why kill over that shit?"

"Unless it's way more valuable than rat kibble."

Jac spoke up. "We need to know what is in those boxes delivered yesterday."

Becky shook her head. "Locked down, remember?"

Levi spoke over the video, "Since when has that stopped us?"

"I can go on a recon mission after dark if Sharlee or Kaden can take care of the cameras and alarms."

"I can take care of the alarms. I know the code and my fingerprints are everywhere."

A chorus of male voices spoke in stereo. "No."

Jac chimed in. "You aren't putting yourself at risk, Rebecca. We have too many loose ends right now to make it safe for you."

"Fine, a compromise. If you can't figure it out by the time Monroe needs to go, then I'll do it on the ground."

Garrett said, "Deal."

"No, not deal," said Carter.

She turned pleading eyes to Carter and reached for his hand. "We have to finish this mess up. Please let me do this."

Carter ran his hand over his short-cropped hair and down the back of his neck. "If we can make it safe." Becky leaned over and kissed him. Carter deepened it.

"Get a room, guys," teased Levi on the screen.

Callie got their attention. "We have another bit of news that throws another wrench in the works. Becky's mom was very cozy with Monty. They had lunch together yesterday."

The possible implications were clear, but no one wanted to put thoughts into words.

"Right, here are the new assignments. Let's lock this down today, people. By tomorrow morning, I want Rebecca to be confirmed safe and to be able to turn all this evidence and information to the local police and back out. We need to get back to just doing our normal security and bodyguarding. This other shit is annoying."

Jac spent the next fifteen minutes discussing where things looked like they were going and what he wanted people to explore further. "Carter, find out the connection between Mrs. Carrington and Monty Rasher."

"Garrett, you organize the groundwork there, and we'll touch base later today."

Carter hesitated. "The Carrington Rasher connection might be delicate."

"No, it's fine. I'm having the conversation anyway. Might as well get what we need in the process," said a determined Becky.

They disconnected, and Garrett pulled out his cell and was soon talking on there. "Sharp. Got a minute? We need some assistance."

THE CONVERSATION WITH her mom was difficult. Carter and Becky sat in the kitchen with Candace who was more than a little upset about everything. Becky told her about Monty's white truck and their suspicions. The others were going to try to get verification.

"Mom, I know you were with Monty at lunch yesterday."

Candace looked over at James who seemed to track a little better today. "Well, he's a nice man and since your father was gone for the day, you and your friends were busy, I thought I'd accept his lunch invitation."

"Mom, why would he even ask you to lunch? He works for Dad, and you're married."

Candace shrugged and teared up a little. "It started as just some little conversations one day when I brought your dad his coffee thermos and lunch. Then we would talk about other things besides business and soon, we were having the occasional lunch. He's the one who gets your father his special coffee. I had a hard time finding a distributor, so Monty found one and was able to purchase a bunch wholesale. He keeps it in a cool basement and brings me some whenever I run out. That is so considerate. I paid for it of course, but still, it's very nice of him. I'm such a fool."

"Dad drinks a special coffee?"

James stepped into the kitchen. "I don't have to drink it or anything, but I discovered it at a trade show a few years back and I bought some but ran out. I had no idea that it was difficult to find. I would have been fine without it, Candace."

"It's fancy coffee. I ran out of our coffee today so that's what I made for you. Taste it."

Carter immediately took the cup out of Becky's reach. "Candace, when did he start supplying you with the coffee?"

"Just before...Thanksgiving. Is it the coffee that is affecting your father? I gave it to him. It's not a medical condition." Candace began to cry, and James put his arms around her from the back.

"You weren't to know, dear. But if it's all the same to you, I think I'll stay off the coffee for a while."

"We need all the bags you have of coffee," said Becky.

"He just gave me a new bag yesterday." She pulled it out and handed it to Carter.

"Dad, call your accountant. I was going to drop off the paperwork but tell him you'll have the inventory in another day or two. I think we can figure all of this out soon."

James nodded. "Then I'll go see Karl in the hospital. They say Bobby's brother shot him. Can you believe it?"

Later that evening it turned out the Candace conversation was much more difficult than getting into the warehouse because, at dinner, James received a call that said the cops were done with it. With no one else knowing it was released, it was the optimal time for them to get in.

Getting in to open the boxes was easy but what they found left them confused for a few moments. The boxes were filled with repackaged, loose rat food pellets. The pellets were larger than standard pellets, but down in the center of the box was crystal meth. They took a box to have it tested but no one had any doubt.

With the other information that Garrett, Monroe, and Callie had discovered, it was time to go back to Lexington. Mystery solved.

Chapter 17

M ark walked in with a waddling but healthy-looking Jessie. "Jessica Ashley Jensen, this isn't a race. They will wait for us."

"Mark, you have called me Ashley for the last time. I told you my middle name, verified by my birth certificate, is Jessica *Ashlynn*. Which, of course, doesn't matter if you never used my middle name, but since it is one of the things you do, could you learn to say it right?"

Mark's face was a little pinched and the plastered-on expression of his long-suffering during these last days told everyone there would be three in the Jensen household at any moment.

"You are beautiful," said Carter, always the first on the team to notice the women in a comforting, admiring way. He was rewarded with a gracious smile from Jessie and a death stare from Mark. Carter smiled. He got what Mark was feeling even though he knew there was nothing to fear from any of the men in this room.

The only woman in their group that Carter had ever lusted after sat grumpily next to him. She'd been moody lately and Carter was beginning to suspect why but he was not ready to share. Instead, he ignored Becky and stood to help support Jessie falling to a firm and yet comfortable chair. They'd all learned when Sharlee was pregnant that at this stage of the game, anything too soft would find them unable to get up from that spot when the frequent bathroom urges came and each time you helped them out of their seat they would be rewarded with not a demure thank you but a complaint about the seating.

Sharlee and Ivy brought out the whiskey she was trying. "Johnny Walker Blue Label. I know you think it might be too domestic but it's good."

When the bathroom size Dixie cups came around, Becky made a little face. "I'm not sure I'll like whiskey."

"Probably not. There is some virgin daiquiri mixed with fruit. You want some of that, Baby Bear?"

Becky relaxed. Carter smiled. That sounded better to both of them. When Garrett brought her drink he leaned down between Carter and Becky. "Something we should know?"

Becky smiled sadly and nodded. "I hate hard liquor straight."

Garrett stood back up and laughed. "Noted."

Once Jessie was settled, the rest rearranged to find a spot in the spacious room. Jac's operation room was supposed to be another living space, like a den or office or even library but it was now accommodating the closest people in his life. Carter looked around and realized these people were the core of his and Becky's life. They breathed in sync.

Today, like in the past weeks, was about Rebecca. It was time to lay out the mess in nice, neat lines and Carter sat back next to his darling woman whom he planned on proposing to and marrying before the month was out. Becky didn't think Carter noticed things and to be honest, he didn't notice everything, but he was observant, especially anything concerning the love of his life. Becky's period was very important to him since he'd taken her without protection. He was still waiting for her menses. Definitely time for a ring.

"Okay, people, let's get this all laid out. You know the drill. We all know the players, or most of them, so I won't bore you with that bit, just to say this one was a little bit challenging in that there were more elements than we usually deal with. So, incident by incident. Charlotte and Kaden, you have the floor."

Sharlee stood up and moved to the computer keyboard and Kaden walked to another one. Up went all the names and pictures of everyone involved.

"Okay," started Kaden, "We were worried about Ramirez's part in all this but while he does factor in, it was not of his doing. So he is out of the frame for any of this." Kaden moved Ramirez to the side of the screen. He looked over at Becky, "Sorry, Becky, it wasn't him."

Becky nodded. Sharlee highlighted Karl. "I know we all had focused on Karl being the culprit, but he was more a victim. He is responsible for part of this, though. Now this is where it gets interesting. Becky?"

"Okay, the first incident, the snowplow. The key that unlocked that event was from the white truck. We got it on a street cam, and as it passed Ivy and Kaden's. I had the impression it was familiar, but..." she shrugged, "Not familiar enough to jog my memory."

Callie jumped in. "Until you were shot at."

"Right. Then both Sharlee, as she was viewing through the security cameras, and I noticed that the white truck that Monty had was the truck in the video and that I remembered from that night. So now Monty, the warehouse manager, is in the frame."

"So, while Jessie and I were working on the inventory snafu, the rest of you were working on other things. Thanks so much, Jessie. It was part of the untangling that got us here."

Jessie grinned. "It was fun and *not* boring."

Mark nodded and gave Jessie a raised eyebrow. "And I appreciate that it didn't require her to leave home."

"The second incident," said Carter with a grimace, "Was the car bomb."

Garrett nodded. "Right, and Nick Sharp told us what he found, and the trace elements of things that go in pet feed sent us back to Becky's family business and the question of whom the car bomb was intended for."

Carter added. "We never suspected Becky's dad because he was having problems with his memory. It would have needed someone with a sharp brain to execute the building and attaching of the device. More about that soon. Thanks, Garrett, for jumping in and taking care of my girl."

"Becky was our first..." Garrett smiled, "Employee. She's special to us all." He redirected when Carter shot him the death glare. "Besides, Nick listened to him, and he didn't have the technological or mechanical understanding to put it together easily. So he was out of the frame."

Becky smiled. "Yeah, he never could help with my science projects."

"So, onto the next event," said Jac. "The boat parade." He grumbled because his family was put at risk, and, as everyone knew, no one fucked with his family.

"Right," said Monroe, "next comes the Ramirez affair. Becky was given tampered water from what looked like a temp-hire. Who it actually turned out to be was... Our new suspect, please. Yes, this gentleman by the name of Carlos Bandera, the son of a close associate of Ramirez, Montenegro Bandera. His son wasn't a server that night. He was there under the guise of a guest to get Becky to stop digging into the inventory numbers at the warehouse."

"Hey, wait, that is the warehouse worker that helps Monty."

"Yes, it is. So now we are back to the warehouse connection," said Monroe.

Carter jumped back in. "Now to the last event. The trip to Oak Ridge."

"No, I got a threatening phone call."

"Yep, going to get there at the end. Now, the warehouse."

Callie raised her hand. "I can fill in some of this. So, on the day of the shooting, after dropping her dad's thermos off at his store and doing some unproductive snooping, we stopped for lunch. We found Becky's mom leaving the restaurant with the warehouse manager, Monty, and they were obviously familiar with each other." Becky gave Callie a grimace laced with a sad smile.

Carter added. "When we went to the warehouse after lunch to try to work through what the inventory was that had no invoices and found a delivery truck unloading small boxes marked, you guessed it, pet food...rodent pellets."

"And stocking the shelves," added Becky. "Unless you are a food company that has that in your contract, like a brand delivery who fronts the merchandise, then a delivery truck just delivers. It had already been signed as received by Monty Rasher, but no sign of him or my uncle."

Carter jumped back in. "We didn't know if it was explosives or drugs, but likely one of them. We got out of there fast, so we weren't in danger nor caught with the shipment."

"Then it got interesting," said Callie. "I was on the phone getting more information when Carter and Becky were coming out of the warehouse. Carter indicated it was time to go. I was ending my call with Sharlee when there was a shot and Carter yelling. Sharlee did her thing on the cameras while I did mine with the shooter." She shrugged. "It was all good."

"The shooter was Karl's part-time clerk's older brother Royce." Kaden added his picture.

"Fuck," said Levi.

"Right. So then we found my uncle shot in his office, so it wasn't him behind this."

"Partly," said Garrett.

Jac stood in front of everyone, and he acted like he was a game show host with answers that the participants, in this case, his people, answered randomly.

"To begin with, the plane incident that I was trying to link to any of this shit has no link. It was a random or targeted act of sabotage by someone who had access to the hangar, whether by our carelessness or previous access, I don't know, but the security end has been upgraded and adjusted. That won't happen again." Jac shook his head.

"Thank God for that," Carter said.

"The reason the truck incident happened was our little band of criminals discovered that Becky was not happy with the inventory when her dad told the warehouse worker Carlos,

Monty, and Karl. All part of the crime in progress. So, it was just their dumb luck that it played out the way it did. Royce was behind the wheel, under orders from his boss, to take care of the problem and there was no further plan. Monty told us that part. Then Monty got the information that Becky was at a friend's party that night from her mom in conversation," said Garrett.

"Who is the ringleader?" asked Mallory.

"Who is connected but never got his hands dirty?" asked Jac.

"There isn't anyone," said Mark.

"Wrong. So let me finish. The attempt was unsuccessful, and Becky didn't stop diving into the inventory mess, so they needed to try again. Her car."

"Okay," said Monroe, "Tell us about the car bomb."

Jac continued. "It was Royce who planted the device. After the shooting, we identified him on the camera, and he confessed from the hospital. So that mystery is solved. He did it at the direction of his boss."

"Which you still aren't going to tell us," said Callie.

"Hold on. So now to the boat parade."

Mark nodded. "Right, that was done by Carlos, the warehouse worker who is also the son of Ramirez's business associate."

Jac nodded. "Yes, he was in with the group and has joined his buddies in jail. Then there was the phone call. That was traced to a burner phone, but it was sold in Tennessee, so we can assume it was someone that Becky had not met because she didn't recognize the voice, and it didn't seem disguised."

"Next comes the warehouse," said Levi.

Jac leaned against Sharlee's computer desk. "Okay, hold on-to your seats. Royce's part, as we can see, was lackey. He did the truck run, the phone call, and the shooting. Nice shot, by the way, Callie."

Callie grinned. "No one shoots at my family."

Kaden said, "Damn straight."

"Okay, so now we go on to Carlos. He had a connection to Ramirez and likely learned of the event and the guest list from his father, who was invited. So he attends with his parent and dresses so he can easily drop the jacket and look like a server. He does the deed, then when it didn't happen as quickly as he needed it to, he bailed, threw back on his jacket, and pretended just to be returning from the head."

"Not the boss, then," said Ivy.

"Nope. But he did discover that Monty was skimming profits by selling to direct customers out of the warehouse, and so he blackmailed him to store more goods, drugs, in the ware-house. All initiated by his boss."

"Then, onto Karl, who was selling illegal exotic animals from his home for the last few years."

Becky looked at Jessie. "That's where all his money came from."

"Yep, but it gets better. When Karl discovered Monty sell-ing things out of the warehouse and noticed the new boxes, he opened one and dumped it out. Having been discovered, Mon-ty tells Karl that if he wants to continue his exotic trade, then he needs to look the other way with the boxes. They pay Karl's storage fee to Becky's father, but that's it."

"Now everyone is tied to everyone and yanking the leash when things are just right. It is definitely a house of cards they had going on. Becky could have brought everything down," said Carter.

"And, eventually, did," said Jac. "So now I have accounted for all the players, but there are some extras we need to add in. In November, when James began to suspect something was going on, he confided in his brother, who let the information flow along the food chain. Monty needed to get him to stop, so when he found out about the special coffee that was his in. Candace had mentioned she wanted to get it for her husband but was finding it difficult for retail customers to get hold of it. He put in a warehouse order and gave it to her, one bag at a time, meaning he would have access to what Candace knew about things when he dropped the next bag, or took her to the occasional lunch."

"I get it. The more your dad was checked out, the more your mom looked for companionship. It was really ingenious," said Sharlee.

Jac continued. "He poisoned the coffee with a very low dose of Rohypnol. Because it was distributed unevenly in the coffee, some days were more or less fuzzy for James. That kept him out of the inventory problem. Since he only drank that coffee at work, his weekends were better.

"That's why he was fuzzy. Mom was putting the coffee in his thermos. She isn't a coffee drinker, so that she wouldn't have been at risk. That's where they got where I lived. Mom must have told them enough for them to find me."

"Finally, the end. Who is the damn ringleader?"

"Robert "Bobby" Morton."

"What? Royce's brother?" Becky stood up. "He is always nice to me. He wouldn't try to kill me or hurt my dad."

"Bobby got in over his head as a teenager. You may have remembered that Karl took him in during high school to keep an eye on him and help give him some legal money. Well, he never let go of the connections and was selling meth at college. When he discovered that Karl was doing exotic animals last year, he used that as a springboard and insurance to get things done. The only one who knew that he was the ringleader, running the show, was his brother Royce."

"Until Becky fixed his wagon," said Carter, who kissed her.

"Until Becky got help from all of you. I would have given up and likely lost my father and mother in the process. I can't thank you all enough."

"No thanks necessary. You're family, and this is a family business, so you need to get back to work." The room erupted in laughter and playful teasing.

"Yes, sir."

"Not until Monday. I have someplace we need to go this weekend."

Jac sighed. "Already looking for another vacation? Fine. Monday it is."

"Fucking hate that word."

Jac and Mark spoke at the same time. "Language!"

DINNER WAS OVER AND cleaned away. Spring and Florent took off to Spring's favorite restaurant for their own dinner, and as they were exiting the front door, Spring stopped.

"Oh, Mr. Reynaud."

"Jac. I keep telling you to call me Jac. You live in my home. You're part of my family. You call me Jac." His demeanor and tone told her he was earnest.

"Jac, when you were in your meeting, the gate security delivered a note that was sent to the house. I left it on the tray." She pointed to the envelope and waved goodbye as Florent swept her through the front door.

Jac picked up the envelope. His friends were gathering their coats to leave, but when they saw the envelope, they gathered around him.

Garrett spoke. "Is it what we think it is?"

Jac grimaced. "Probably." He opened the envelope bare-handed. Experience had taught them that there were never any prints left behind but theirs.

"*You didn't invite me to your party and went on a trip without me. Guess I'll have to gate crash.*"

Mark yelled into the hallway. "Jessie just broke her water and has had her first real contraction. We are having a baby, thank God!"

The room was activated. Sharlee brought out a towel from the bathroom. "Trust me. You will need it."

They helped Jessie with her coat and then helped Mark get Jessie in the car. After they had headed down the driveway, the rest gathered their things. It was going to be a long, exciting night.

Epilogue

A new baby girl was exciting. Becky had always felt part of the group as they grew, but there had been something missing. She didn't feel it anymore. She had witnessed Sharlee's new baby, but now with the other women around, it felt like she was on the outside a little. With all they had just gone through, Becky knew she was part of everyone and everything this amazing group did, and yet...

Looking at the red, scrunched-up face of the newest member of their family, Anora Jensen slept peacefully as she was introduced to every member of her loving family. Her adoring fans spoke over themselves.

"She's gorgeous."

"Perfect."

"How do you raise a girl?"

The comments kept coming, and her parents, while tired, were over the moon. Mark was already watch-guarding his baby girl, as it should be.

Jessie looked over at Jac. "You don't need me for a month, so Becky will have to ride roughshod over the finance department. I'll be offline."

"And only reachable by phone for the month after that," said Mark.

"Of course. No worries, Mark," said Becky. "Jessie and I have it all figured out."

She chose not to tell him that she and Jessie had already set up how they would stay in touch as necessary. No need to bother him with those details.

Everyone went home for a well-deserved three-day weekend, content with the knowledge that all was right in their world.

Except for those damn cards.

CARTER LOOKED AT BECKY and couldn't believe she was his woman. She'd gone through some trying weeks, but here she was, gazing at him with adoring eyes as she undressed in front of him, giving him a show. She would occasionally feel dissatisfied with her body, but he would make it his mission, one of many, to make sure she knew how attracted he was to all of her.

His cock was hard as stone. He knew Becky was wet for him. She had taken off her panties, and he reached out his hand for them. She never wavered but dropped them in his hand.

He sniffed, and her pupils dilated.

"You smell so fucking good. I need to taste."

Becky shook her head. "I haven't showered."

"Oh, baby girl. You did not just try to tell your Daddy no, did you?"

She simply stared at him. Her hands roamed her body, driving him wild. She kept her eyes on him as he reached for her. Loving her was easy and intense. He needed that. So did she.

"Come here, baby, Daddy needs to touch you."

He held his hand out to her, watching as she confidently took it, coming to him and putting her arms around his neck. His body ached with need. He could feel her tremble with her own desperation as he ravaged her mouth with his, tasting her essence, inhaling her delicate honeysuckle scent that enhanced her personal fragrance.

"I need more, Daddy. Touch me. Take me, Carter," she pleaded, her breathing growing shallow and raspy.

"I know what you need, baby, I know. I need you too. Please know I'll always be here for you, always need you this way."

Carter placed his hands on her broad, luscious hips and manipulated her to bend over the bed, face down on the bedding, her ass in the air.

"This is going to be fast and furious, baby. I can't wait long." He caressed her ass cheeks, kissing, pinching, smacking. He loved the way her ass was so needy. Her pussy was dripping. He reached out his hand to her drenched sanctum. Her cry of want echoed in her movements as she pushed her undulating pussy into his hand. He groaned. Her ass was so perfect for him. He brought his hand from her pussy and moved them both over her lushness, squeezing her flesh, pulling her cheeks apart to make way for his tongue as he licked her anus, spearing it with his tongue. Her cry of desperation made his cock thicken even more, reaching out to the source of relief.

He stood back just enough to run his finger into her wet channel. Two fingers at once penetrated her back entrance, and his other hand reached for her clit, pinching hard. Her scream was immediate. She pushed her ass hard against his fingers, breeching her own ass, spearing her own body hard. He forced three fingers, it would be painful, but she wanted that bite of pain, needed it.

Carter pulled out his drenched hand from where she'd creamed over it and tasted the ambrosia.

That wet hand slapped her bottom hard as he forced his fingers into her back entrance again. Her cry of pleasurable pain made precum drip from his cock. He couldn't wait any longer. He didn't give her a chance to relax before he was inside of her.

"Is this what you need, baby? Do you need my cock buried inside of your scorching pussy?"

"Yessss." Her breath was fast, shallow, and labored.

"Feel me inside? Grab me, hold me, caress that cock as I ram you and take your ass with my hand. I'll take it soon with my thick, pulsing cock. I'll show no mercy, and you won't want me to. Feel me."

Her hand reached back and encircled his hot, thrusting member, making things messier and hotter. Damn, she was so sexy. She screamed again, and he withdrew his fingers from her ass and watched the muscles of her anus grope for him to refill it. He leaned down to use his tongue. He was going to blow. Soon he would take her ass completely, but now he would grab his release.

He grasped her fleshy hips and pounded himself into her, listening to her whimper and cry her third release. That was his cue. He slammed in hard, slapping her ass as he released. No condom. No barrier. She wasn't on birth control now. He knew she was likely already pregnant, but if she wasn't, he wanted to give his love her heart's desire.

He would always give her what she needed.

He kissed down her back, and slowly, they came back to themselves. He kissed her back, then stood from his bent position over her prostrate body. Leaving to clean himself up, he returned to clean her before bringing her up to the center of the bed. Loving how she cuddled into him as though he could meet all her desires. Provide all her needs. That was his mission in life: to be all she would ever need.

"I love you, Rebecca Shea. Will you marry this mean Daddy that loves you with every atom of his being?"

She nodded as though that was all the energy she could muster. "Will you love me this way forever?"

"I'll love you even more."

"Carter, my love, my own Daddy, I'll marry you."

"I will love you until the day I die and beyond, Baby Bear."

"And I love you totally. You are all I need, Daddy, all I will ever need."

The End

About the Author
Alyssa Bailey

USA Today Bestselling Author of Sassy Romance that is realistic and sensual with a touch of suspense. A dyed-in-the-wool Texan living in Alaska for half her life, Alyssa now divides her time between the beauty of Southeast Alaska and the Piney Woods of Northeast Texas. She enjoys taking from her own experiences to create series in fictitious worlds sure to tease the reader's palate and invite them to sink into exciting adventures.

Alyssa enjoys writing consensual power exchanges between intelligent, sassy women who are not afraid to make a stand and loving men confident enough to give their woman space but masterful enough to keep her indulged and protected. There is *always* a "happily ever after."

Visit me online and sign up for my Newsletter:
http://alyssabailey.com[1]
Join my Facebook Group for fun and prizes:
Lazy Days and Romance

---

1. http://alyssabailey.com/

Other Books By Alyssa Bailey

Safe and Secure Series: Contemporary, suspense, spicy
Saving Sharlee (re-release 2023)
Saving Jessie (re-release 2023)
Saving Ivy
Saving Mallory
Saving Callie
Saving Becky
Saving Finley (2023)

CLEARWATER RANCH TRILOGY -Contemporary,
Spicy
Piper's Plan (re-release 2024)
Camille's Second Chance (re-release 2024)
Josie's Refuge

DARLING DUCHESSES: Regency, Daddy Dom, Spicy
The Devil Duke's Little Distraction
The Daring Duke's Little Impulse

GUARDIANS OF REFUGE (Contemporary, Military, Spicy)

    SEAL of Refuge
    The Strategy of Love
    The Tactics of Love
    The Mandate of Love

SAGE COUNTY (Cowboy, Contemporary, Spicy)

    Deep Waters
    Still Waters

IN THE SPIRIT OF CHRISTMAS -Contemporary, Sweet
    Christmas Wishes and You

ANTHOLOGIES (HEAT VARIES)

    Sweet Town Love
    Historical Heroes
    Hero to Obey (limited time)
    Cowboy for a Cause (limited time)
    Naughty 12 Days of Christmas 2017

MULTI-AUTHOR BOX SETS (Heat Level Various)

    Love, Christmas 2 Recipes
    Irresistible Heroes
    Sweet and Sassy Summertime Vol. 2

Dear Santa: A Christmas Wish
Sweet and Sassy New Beginnings

These books will be re-released soon...

Lords and Little Ladies: **Georgian Historical, spicy**
Lord Thayer's Choice
Lord Ashton's Decision
The Black Laird Requires
Lord Kendrick's Obligation

CHASE ABBEY SERIES: Regency, Spicy, Suspense
Lord Barrington's Minx
Becoming Lady Barrington
Lady Caroline's Defiance
His Improper Lady

THE O'CONNOR SERIES: Contemporary, Rancher, Saga, Spicy
Liam & Jocelyn's Story
Her Sweet Complication
Liam's Lessons
Loving Liam

CIARÁN AND KATHERINE'S Story
His Gentle Persuasion
Rancher's Creed
Katie Consents

QUINLAN AND CHEYENNE'S Story
Quinlan's Quest
Accepting His Way
Her Balancing Act

KELLI AND PARKER'S Story
Meeting Her Needs
Kissing Kelli
Keeping Kelli

CIÁN AND MOLLY'S STORY
In Pursuit of Molly
Freeing Molly
Forever Molly

LONE WIND SERIES: Contemporary, spicy Native American
Reclaiming Clover

TAMING TEXANNA -American Historical, Native American, Spicy

    Cowboy Welcome- Contemporary, Spicy

Alyssa Bailey written as Tasha Winters

To Be Re-Released Soon...

CAPTURED SERIES-URBAN Fantasy/Time Travel
Captured Obedience
Captured Desire

ALPHAS IN THE WILD
Wild Alpha Fantasy
Wild Alpha Promise

Don't miss out!

Visit the website below and you can sign up to receive emails whenever Alyssa Bailey publishes a new book. There's no charge and no obligation.

https://books2read.com/r/B-A-MXIL-QZJIC

BOOKS 2 READ

Connecting independent readers to independent writers.

Did you love *Saving Becky*? Then you should read *Saving Callie* by Alyssa Bailey!

Loyalty is good, but blind loyalty is deadly.

Garrett Sullivan and Katrina Long, known as Callie to Garrett and friends due to her California beach upbringing was in a serious dating arrangement. He loved her. They argued over her taking an undercover job with Homeland Security into the dark underworld of the Mexican Mafia in Southern California. The next evening there was a note from Callie saying her dad was sick and she'd call when she got there. She never called.

After a year of pounding her family and Homeland for information where his girl was, his team found her but she slipped away when approached. Soon afterwards Garrett was told she was dead but he never believed it. Now, three years later, Sharlee received a call from Callie who was in trouble but disconnected before Sharlee could trace her. Garrett's primary goal was to get Callie to safety and after that, he didn't know.

Within a week, Homeland wanted him to lead a team for a local job two years after Callie's old employers had tried hard to distance themselves from him. Something fishy was going on and Garrett and teammates would figure it out but in the meantime, they would find and save Callie from whatever danger she was in before it was too late.

Read more at alyssabailey.com.

Also by Alyssa Bailey

Safe and Secure
Saving Becky

Watch for more at alyssabailey.com.